BLOOD AND LOYALTY!
From The Teen Motherhood To The Queen Of The Street

TEAMA HERICE

DEDICATION

To my extraordinary husband, Wickly –

You are my anchor, my confidant, and the steady heartbeat of our family. Your love is the safe harbor I return to, no matter how far my dreams take me. Thank you for carrying me through sleepless nights, wild ideas, and the countless times I doubted myself. Your faith in me never wavered, and because of that, I have learned to believe in myself even more. You are my forever blessing, my partner in every sense of the word, and I love you endlessly.

To my remarkable oldest son, Justin –

From the moment you came into this world, you've carried wisdom far beyond your years. You've shown me that strength doesn't always roar; sometimes, it's found in quiet leadership and in the way you love your family with such fierce devotion. You are not only a big brother but a hero in your own right, and I could not be prouder of the man you are becoming. Your light makes this world brighter, and I'm grateful to be your mom.

To my sweet baby boy, Tyson –

This book is your story, your legacy, your proof that courage wears many faces—even the face of a child with a heart too big for fear to hold. You remind me daily that love and bravery are the strongest forces we have. Every word I've written carries a piece of you in it, because you, my son,

are my inspiration, my joy, and my reminder that even the smallest voices can echo the loudest truths.

To my radiant nieces, Maniece and Li'Byra –

You are laughter in motion, creativity uncontained, and pure magic in human form. Watching you blossom into bold, brilliant young women has been one of my greatest joys. You embody resilience, grace, and fire, and I pray you always know how cherished you are. This world is wide and waiting for your sparkle—never dim it for anyone.

To my family—my circle of strength, love, and endless inspiration—

Every page of this book was born from you, for you, and because of you. You are my roots and my wings, my reason and my why. May these words serve as a reminder that you are extraordinary, you are powerful, and above all—you are deeply, unshakably loved.

With all my love,

TeAma Herice

ABOUT THE AUTHOR

TeAma Herice is a proud wife, devoted mother, and passionate creative whose heart beats for children, family, and faith. With strong values and an even stronger village, TeAma believes in the power of storytelling to inspire, uplift, and affirm readers of all ages.

Her debut children's book, Tyson's Big Brave Heart, was inspired by her youngest son and is a tribute to every child learning to be brave in their own way. Through this story, TeAma encourages families to embrace courage, love, and self-worth, reminding children that even the smallest voices deserve to be heard and celebrated.

She followed with her second book, Ain't No Brakin Us, a powerful tale of resilience, love, and perseverance that captures the determination to overcome life's obstacles and hold on to what truly matters.

Now, with her third release, Blood Loyalty, TeAma takes readers into a gripping world of family, betrayal, and unshakable bonds. This novel explores how loyalty is tested when trust is broken, and whether love and truth can survive the ultimate trials.

When she's not writing, TeAma pours her creativity into her business, Just In Time Accessories, or enjoys life's simple joys with her loving husband Wickly and their two amazing sons, Justin and Tyson. Every project she touches—whether storytelling or entrepreneurship—is rooted in faith, family, and purpose.

TeAma is excited to share that more books are on the horizon, each one crafted to touch hearts, spark conversations, and leave lasting impressions.

Website: www.cantputdown.com
Email: cantputdown01@gmail.com
Instagram: @teama01
Facebook: @Teama.copeland1

ACKNOWLEDGMENTS

Whew—what a journey this has been! Writing Blood Loyalty and bringing it into the world didn't just come from a place of imagination—it came from deep love, faith, and the unshakable encouragement of the people God placed in my life.

To my bestie, my forever friend, Herman "Junior" Callwood –

What would life be without your laugh, your wisdom, and your ability to keep it real even when I don't want to hear it? You've walked with me through every high, every low, and every "Sis, you got this" moment. Thank you for being my safe place, my sounding board, my family. You've held me down, lifted me up, and pushed me forward when I wanted to give up. I cherish our bond more than words could ever express. Mushed up for life!

To my brother in spirit and literary fire, Anthony P. Brown –

Whew! Where do I even begin? Your success lit a fire in me. Watching you write, publish, and boldly share your truth gave me the courage to step into mine. You never let me doubt myself for long—you reminded me that my voice matters, my stories matter, and that I was created for this. Your push, your example, your encouragement—it all broke through my fear and birthed books. Thank you for not just opening the door but holding it wide open for me to walk through.

To my sister-friend, Charmaine Brown –

There are friends, and then there are sisters chosen by the heart. Charmaine, you are that for me. Your love, encouragement, and belief in me has been a blessing beyond measure. You celebrate my wins like they're your own, pray for me when I don't even ask, and remind me of my worth when the noise of doubt gets too loud. Thank you for being that consistent, genuine, and uplifting presence in my life. Our bond is a gift, and I honor you for standing with me through it all.

To my angel in heaven, my beloved sister, Byra Copeland –

Not a day goes by that I don't feel your presence, guiding me, comforting me, pushing me to keep going. You were more than a sister—you were my protector, my confidant, my cheerleader, and my example of strength.

Losing you left a space in my heart that can never be filled, but your spirit lives on in every step I take. When I sit down to write, I hear your voice reminding me to keep pushing, to keep dreaming, to keep shining. This book is for you, Byra. I carry your love with me always, and I pray that every word I write makes you proud up there in heaven. You are my angel, my light, my forever inspiration.

To everyone who believed in me, supported me, read my drafts, shared my posts, or simply asked, "How's the book coming?" — thank you. Your words kept me writing on the days I felt like quitting.

And to every reader who picks up this book—to every family, every friend, every person navigating loyalty, love, and life's toughest challenges—this book was created for you. My hope is that it touches your heart, opens

your mind, and reminds you that even through betrayal, struggle, and pain, there is always strength, there is always faith, and there is always love.

This journey has been powered by faith, fueled by family, and sustained by a village of love and support. From the depths of my heart, thank you.

With all my love and gratitude,

TeAma Herice

TABLE OF CONTENT

Chapter One
"Fifteen and On Her Own"

The Florida sun wasn't friendly that morning. It hit hard against Jazmine's skin as she stood on the front porch of her mama's three-bedroom houseoff Sistrunk Boulevard, her six-month-old son shifting in her arms. Theporch boards creaked beneath her Nike slides, same ones she'd been rocking since eighth grade. Her backpack hung off one shoulder, packed with more diapers than books.

Inside, her mama's voice sliced through the humid air, sharp like a slap.

"I told you last night, Jazmine! You ain't finna have me raising no damn baby while you out tryna be cute at school or chasing behind some fool!"

Jazmine bit the inside of her cheek. "I ain't chasing nobody, Ma. I'm going to school—"

Her mama stormed to the doorway, arms folded, her face tight with frustration. "Don't play me. You got a baby now. You wanna act grown? Be grown. Take care of your child — by yourself. This ain't no daycare, and I ain't no free babysitter!"

Jazmine adjusted Josiah on her hip, his tiny hand gripping one of her long braids. "I'm trying, Ma. I'm really trying."

"Try harder." Her mama's eyes darted down the street, like she was already done with the conversation. "And don't think you got a place to come back to if you can't handle your damn responsibilities."

For a long minute, Jazmine stood there — her, her son, and the heat pressing down on them like a weight.

That afternoon, she sat on the back steps of John I. Leonard High, Josiah's stroller parked beside her, half-empty baby bottle tucked in the cup holder. She should've been in English class, but right now, school felt like a world she didn't belong to anymore.

Groups of girls strolled by, laughing about prom dates and new sneakers. Boys posted up near the gym, cracking jokes. Nobody said nothing to her.

The same girl who used to rock the freshest kicks and keep her nails done was now the girl with a baby and a backpack full of Similac samples.

She pulled out her cracked phone, thumb hovering over Keisha's message.

Keisha: I got a spot if you need a place 2 crash. Hit me.

Simple. Straight. No pity.

Jazmine looked down at Josiah, his big brown eyes watching her, trusting her in a way nobody else ever would.

If the world wanted to throw her out, fine. She'd find her way — for him.

Jazmine stared at the text on her screen for what felt like forever. I got a spot if you need a place 2 crash.

She read it again, then again, until the words started to blur.

Her fingers hovered over the screen, shaking just a little. Not from fear — not anymore. From the weight of it all pressing down on her chest. The truth was, she ain't have no choice. Her mama had made that clear. The door wasn't just shut; it was locked, deadbolted, and sealed with every bitter word they'd thrown at each other over the past six months.

Josiah stirred in the stroller beside her, letting out a soft whimper. She leaned over, gently tucking his blanket around his tiny legs. "I got you, lil man," she whispered. "It's me and you now."

Her thumb finally moved.

Jazmine: Where u at? The reply came back almost instantly.

Keisha: Downtown. You good?

Jazmine stared down the empty hallway behind the school, the weight of the moment hitting her full force. This wasn't no sleepover. This wasn't running away for a night and sneaking back in the morning.

This was the moment her life split in two. Before… and after.

With a deep breath, Jazmine stood up, slinging her backpack over her shoulder. The straps cut into her skin, but she didn't flinch.

She wrapped her fingers around the stroller handle, glancing one last time at the school she barely belonged to anymore.

She didn't know where the road was taking her. But she knew one thing for damn sure… She wasn't turning back.

Chapter Two
"Ain't No Love in These Streets"

The city hit different when you had nowhere to go.

Jazmine stood on the corner of Broward and Andrews Avenue, watching the early evening crowd pulse through downtown Fort Lauderdale. Businessmen in suits. College girls in sundresses. Hustlers perched on street corners like kings without a throne.

She blended with none of them.

Josiah whimpered in his stroller, his tiny hands reaching for something only he could see. Jazmine knelt beside him, brushing a kiss across his forehead. "We good, baby. We gon' be good."

A horn beeped twice. She looked up to see Keisha's red Honda Civic crawling through traffic, the bass rattling so hard it made heads turn. Keisha leaned across the passenger seat, shades pulled down just enough to show her eyes.

"Get in, girl."

Jazmine folded up the stroller with practiced hands, her heart thudding as she tucked it in the trunk alongside her backpack. This wasn't no sleepover. This was her whole life, packed into the back of a beat-up Civic.

She slid into the passenger seat, cradling Josiah against her chest.

Keisha gave her a quick once-over. "You good?"

Jazmine locked eyes with her in the mirror. "I'm straight."

Keisha smirked, sliding the car into gear. "Yeah… You will be."

Keisha's spot sat in a dusty complex on the west side — one of those places where the paint peeled off the walls, the porch lights barely worked, and the front gate was permanently broken.

But the rent was paid. The locks worked. And for Jazmine, it was everything she needed.

Inside, the apartment smelled like a mix of cocoa butter, flat irons, and yesterday's blunt. A small two-bedroom, furnished with mismatched pieces and a couch that sank in the middle.

Keisha waved her toward the second bedroom. "It's small, but it's yours till you figure it out."

Jazmine dropped her backpack in the corner, then laid Josiah down on a folded comforter on the floor. He cooed, staring up at the ceiling fan spinning lazily overhead.

She sat on the edge of the mattress, wiping her hands across her jeans. "I don't know how to thank you for this."

Keisha leaned against the doorframe, arms crossed, nails painted a sharp cherry red. "Don't trip. I been there. Hell, I'm still there." She tilted her head, eyes narrowing. "But you ever thought about getting some real money?"

Jazmine blinked. "What you mean? A job?"

Keisha gave a low chuckle, stepping into the room. "Nah. I'm talking about the streets. Hustling. Moving weight. Running plays. You smart, Jaz. And you got a mouthpiece. You ain't gotta be broke or begging nobody for nothing.

"Jazmine shook her head. "I got a baby, Keish."

Keisha shrugged. "So? That just mean you got a bigger reason to win." She smirked. "Plus, everybody in this game doing it for somebody. Their mama. Their kid. Or their damn self. It ain't for everybody… but if you got the heart?" She leaned in closer. "You could have your own everything."

Jazmine felt something harden inside her chest — something sharp, new, and dangerous.

She thought about her mama's words.

You wanna be grown? Be grown.

She thought about every look, every whisper behind her back at school.

That's the girl with the baby…

She thought about Josiah sleeping on a comforter on the floor of a borrowed room.

She squared her shoulders. "What I gotta do?"

Keisha's smirk stretched into something slow and knowing. "You just took the first step."

That night, when Josiah finally drifted off, Jazmine sat on the edge of the makeshift bed, staring at her reflection in the cracked mirror hanging on the back of the door.

She didn't recognize the girl looking back at her.

This girl's eyes held something sharper. A quiet, cold fire.

Tomorrow, her real education would begin.

And failure?

Wasn't even an option.

Chapter Three
"The First Play"

Morning felt heavy in the air — sticky with the kind of humidity that clung to your skin like bad news.

Jazmine sat on the edge of the mattress, staring down at Josiah. He slept like the world hadn't already started turning its back on them.

She brushed her fingers over his soft curls. "We good, baby boy. Mama got you."

But even as she whispered it, her chest squeezed. Because deep down, she knew — this was about to be a different kind of life.

Keisha's Civic rolled through the city like a shadow. Downtown skyscrapers faded in the rearview as they cut deeper west. Keisha leaned back in her seat, one hand on the wheel, the other flipping through a fat roll of cash held together with a rubber band.

"You sure about this?" Keisha asked, eyes hidden behind blacked-out shades.

Jazmine sat straight, Josiah strapped in the back. "I'm sure."

Keisha let out a slow exhale. "Aight. Streets don't love nobody. You make moves for you and yours. That's it. Keep your head up, your eyes open, and your mouth shut unless you counting money. First rule."

Jazmine nodded, her heart hammering so loud it felt like it echoed in her ears.

They rolled into The Pines — a complex that smelled like sweat, weed, and lost dreams. Rusted cars lined the parking lot. A little girl played double-dutch with a rope that looked like it'd snap any second. An old man posted up on a milk crate nodded as they drove by.

By the stairwell stood Dre — tall, dark, lean, arms cut with muscle, a gold chain catching flashes of sunlight. His eyes locked on them before the car even stopped.

Keisha put the Civic in park. "That's Dre. He good people — long as you don't cross him. You gon' give this to him."

She reached into the glovebox and pulled out a slim envelope. It looked harmless, plain. But Jazmine knew better. That envelope could buy a week's worth of diapers... or ruin your life.

"Tell him Keisha sent you. Don't overthink it. Don't act shook. Handle your business and come back to the car."

Jazmine stared at the envelope, her throat tight. "Why me?"

Keisha gave a slow, knowing smirk. "'Cause you ain't the type they see coming. Pretty face, baby on your hip... they'll never expect it. And that? That's your power."

The second Jazmine stepped out the car, the air changed.

She could feel eyes on her — Dre's, the kids in the lot, even the old man on the crate. The weight of the envelope in her hand pressed against her palm like a dare.

Dre didn't move until she was a few feet away. "You Keisha's lil friend?"

Jazmine nodded once. "Yeah. She sent me.

"He reached out, fingers brushing hers as he took the envelope. His eyes flicked from her face to the street behind her.

"You know what this is, right?"

Jazmine lifted her chin. "I know enough."

Dre gave a slow smirk. "You got heart. But don't get it twisted... the streets'll eat you alive if you let 'em."

She didn't blink. "I don't plan on letting 'em."

Dre gave a short laugh — more like an exhale of respect than amusement. "Bet." He tucked the envelope in his back pocket. "Tell Keisha we straight."

Jazmine nodded and turned back toward the Civic, every step feeling heavier than the last.

She slid back into the passenger seat, her hands surprisingly steady.

Keisha grinned, blowing smoke out the window. "That's my girl. First play done. See? Easy money."

Jazmine glanced at Josiah in the back seat — his chubby cheeks, soft breathing, his tiny hands curled into fists.

She looked at Keisha. "What's next?"

Keisha's smirk deepened. "Now? We teach you the game."

That night, Jazmine sat on the edge of the bed, staring at her reflection in the cracked mirror.

The girl staring back wasn't the scared, kicked-out teenage mom from yesterday.

Her eyes were sharper. Harder.

And deep down, she felt it — a cold spark flickering inside her.

She didn't just survive her first play.

She liked it.

The rush.

The respect.

The power.

Tomorrow wasn't promised.

But tonight... tonight, she wasn't a victim. She was in the game.And the game?

It was just getting started.

Chapter Four
"Baptism by Fire"

By the end of the week, Jazmine had made five drops.

Each one easier than the last

The first time, her hands shook.

By the fifth? She barely blinked.

Money started stacking — twenties, fifties, a few crumpled hundreds folded in her bra. Enough to buy Josiah new clothes, diapers without stressing, and even pay Keisha something for letting her stay.

But Keisha's words echoed in her mind every night.

Ain't no love in this game.

It was a Friday evening when the streets finally showed their teeth.

Keisha dropped her on the corner of 13th and Sunrise, a spot that stayed busy — tourists, locals, out-of-towners who didn't know better. Jazmine had a quick handoff with a dude named Melo — easy money, in and out.

Or so she thought. She was halfway back to the Civic when a black Crown Vic easedaround the corner, creeping low.

Undercover.

The knot in her gut tightened.

Two men in plain clothes stepped out — badges flashing under thin windbreakers.

"Hold up, shorty!" one called, voice loud and sharp.

Jazmine's blood iced over.

For a split second, instinct screamed run.But Keisha's voice echoed in her head — Keep your head up, your eyes open, and your mouth shut unless you counting money.

She turned slowly, face blank, heart racing.

"What's good?" she asked, her voice calm… way calmer than she felt.

The taller cop eyed her hard. "We've had reports of some action around here. You seen anything?"

Jazmine blinked, giving him the same bored look she'd seen Keisha give a hundred dudes. "Nah.

I'm just waiting on my ride."

They looked her up and down — the fresh braids, the baby bag slung over her shoulder, the Jordan slides on her feet.

The shorter one tilted his head. "You sure about that?"

She shrugged. "Y'all see a problem?"

A long pause.

Then the taller one gave a small, almost annoyed nod. "Get off this corner."

Jazmine didn't move too fast. Didn't breathe too hard.

She walked back to the car like her legs weren't jelly.

Once inside, Keisha gave her a slow, side-eye glance. "You good?"
Jazmine stared straight ahead. "Yeah. I'm good."

Keisha nodded, pulling off. "Good. Now you know. This life don't come with warning signs — just lessons."

That night, after Josiah fell asleep, Jazmine sat on the porch of Keisha's apartment, staring into the dark.

The streets had almost swallowed her.

But she didn't fold.

She took a deep breath, her chest rising with something new — not fear… but fire.

She'd just had her baptism by fire.

And now?She was really in the game.

Chapter Five
"Money, Power, Pressure"

Money Changed Everything.

In just a few weeks, Jazmine had gone from making a few small drops to pulling in real money — five, six, sometimes seven hundred in a single night.

And she never touched the product.

She played her lane — a middle runner, a connector.

She learned the names, the faces, the codes.

She learned how to count a stack by feel.

How to watch for unmarked cars in her rearview.

How to clock a snake in a smile.

The first time she peeled off a stack of crisp twenties, she cried.

Quiet tears — the kind you blink away before anybody sees.

She'd walked into Target that morning with Josiah on her hip, bought a pack of Pampers, formula, two packs of onesies, and a new pair of sneakers…

And paid cash.

No EBT.

No handouts.

No sideways looks from cashiers.

She walked out the store with her head high.

That feeling?

It was addicting.

Keisha started giving her more freedom.

"You move smart," Keisha said one night as they counted out bundles at the kitchen table. "You ain't like most chicks. You think."

Jazmine smirked, flipping a stack between her fingers. "I got reasons to think."

Keisha's eyes flicked toward the bedroom, where Josiah slept. "Yeah. You do."

But the streets don't let you eat without testing your hunger.

And the test always comes when you least expect it.

It started with whispers.

A girl she barely knew — Tasha — slid in her DMs late one night.

Tasha: Watch your circle. Everybody ain't solid.

Jazmine stared at the message for a long minute before deleting it.

Then a random number hit her two days later.

Unknown: You moving heavy now huh? Bet. Watch your back.

She brushed it off until Dre brought it up during a pickup.

"You making moves," he said, eyes sharp. "That means people watching."

Jazmine zipped her purse shut, her face cool. "Let 'em watch."

Dre leaned on the hood of his car, lips curling into something between a grin and a warning.

"Being seen ain't the problem," he said. "Being set up is."

Jazmine met his eyes, letting the silence sit heavy between them.

"I ain't worried."

Dre gave a slow nod. "You better not be stupid either."

That night, she sat at the kitchen table counting money — Josiah's soft breathing drifting from the next room.

Five stacks in neat rows. More cash than she ever imagined holding in her hands.

Keisha leaned on the counter, arms folded, watching her.

"You moving fast," Keisha said, her voice low. "That's good… but you know what happens to people who move too fast?"

Jazmine didn't look up. "They win?"

Keisha gave a slow, hollow chuckle. "Sometimes." She straightened up. "Other times… they crash."

Jazmine placed the last stack down and met her eyes. "I don't fold."

Keisha stared at her for a long moment — too long.

Then she smiled. "We gon' see."

But that look…

The way Keisha said it…

It stayed with Jazmine long after the money was counted.

The streets were watching.

But Jazmine was starting to wonder…

If maybe the biggest threat wasn't the streets at all.

Maybe…

It was the people sitting at her own table.

Chapter Six
"Snakes in the Grass"

Jazmine always thought betrayal would come loud — a gun, a fight, some screaming in the streets.

But nah.

It came quiet.

Soft.

Like a whisper slipping in when you least expect it.

It started with the money.

One night, she counted up after a drop with Dre. They'd made a quick flip off a dude from Dania — smooth, clean, in and out.

But when she ran the count back later that night… it was light.

Two-fifty short.

She counted again. Then again. Same.Her first instinct was to check her math.

Second instinct? Look at who touched the money last.

She remembered handing it off to Keisha to break down.

Remembered Keisha telling her, "I'll straighten it out later."

But when Jazmine brought it up again…

Keisha gave her a slick smile. "Girl, it's probably at the bottom of your bag. You stay all over the place."

Jazmine held her stare. "I don't lose count."

Keisha's smile stayed in place — but her eyes went sharp. "Then it's nothing to worry about… right?"

After that, it was Dre.

He started pulling up on her unexpected.

"Just checking in," he'd say, flashing that lazy grin.

But his questions came clipped and loaded.

"How much you holding?"

"Where you going next?"

"You rolling solo?"

At first, she brushed it off as Dre being careful — maybe even a little overprotective.

Until one night, she came around the corner of the complex and caught him leaned up on his car, phone pressed to his ear.

"…Nah, she with me. She don't know nothing yet."

He looked up mid-conversation and locked eyes with her.

For a split second, something passed between them — something cold.

Then Dre slid the phone down and gave her that signature grin. "What up, lil mama? Just business."

Jazmine didn't smile back.

From that night on, she moved different.

Routes changed.

Pickups kept quiet.

Money counted three times before it touched anyone's hands.

She stopped leaving cash in Keisha's house when she wasn't there. Stopped telling Dre anything he didn't need to know.

Her circle got smaller.

Her trust? Damn near nonexistent.

But still… the vibe got heavier.

Keisha started watching her different.

Little glances when Jazmine wasn't supposed to notice.

Weird smiles that didn't reach her eyes.

Extra errands that lined up just a little too perfect with Jazmine's moves.

One night, they sat in the living room — Keisha rolling a blunt, Jazmine scrolling her phone.

Keisha laughed under her breath. "You moving like you don't trust nobody no more."

Jazmine set her phone down slow. "That's how you stay alive out here."

Keisha flicked her lighter, eyes on the flame. "You learning."

Jazmine gave her a thin smile. "Fast learner."

Keisha took a long drag, her gaze never leaving the lighter. "Yeah… I can see that."

Later that night, Jazmine laid in bed with Josiah curled against her chest.

Her heart beat steady, cold.

She wasn't paranoid.

She wasn't imagining things.

The setup wasn't coming.

It was already circling… waiting for the right moment.

But they forgot one thing.

Jazmine didn't fold.

And if they were gonna come for her…

She was gonna be ready.

Chapter Seven
"The Setup"

Friday night air hung thick — humid, sticky, like it knew something foul was in the wind.

Jazmine sat on the edge of Keisha's living room couch, phone pressed to her ear.

Keisha's voice came cool, casual… too casual.

"Got a lil play for you. Easy money. Quick drop-off. Dude off Sistrunk been waiting on it — I told him you'd handle it for me."

Jazmine's eyes narrowed. "Who's the dude?"

Keisha chuckled, like it was funny. "New plug. Melo cousin. He good."

Melo? The same dude who ran sloppy plays and owed everybody on the east?

Yeah… aight.

Jazmine shifted, glancing toward the back room where Josiah slept. "You coming?"

Keisha let a pause stretch before answering. "I would… but Dre gon' roll with you. Y'all got this."

Her stomach flipped — cold, sharp, but she played it cool.

"Bet."

At 10 PM, Dre pulled up in a gray Maxima — windows down, music low, engine humming soft.

He gave her the usual half-grin. "What up, lil mama? You ready?"

Jazmine smirked like nothing was off. "Yeah."

She slid in, bag slung across her chest, heart thudding steady in her ears.

They pulled off.

The ride was quiet — that thick, charged kind of quiet.

Dre kept glancing over at her, like he was checking for cracks in her mask.

Jazmine stayed locked on the window, replaying every sign over the last few weeks in her head like a slow, crawling reel.

The light money.

The weird questions.

Keisha's slick comments.Dre moving funny.

And now this — a late-night drop-off to a dude she ain't never met, with a man she couldn't trust.

Yeah… this wasn't no play.

This was the setup.

They pulled up on 15th and Sistrunk — the block sitting quiet, too quiet for a Friday night.

Dre nodded toward a beat-up duplex with one busted porch light blinking like a warning.

"That's the spot."

Jazmine stared at it.

The house was dead. No music. No cars out front. No lights inside.

"New plug, huh?" she asked, her voice low.

Dre leaned back in his seat, that grin sliding across his face. "Easy money, Jaz. You gon' handle it, or what?"

Her gut screamed.

But her face? Stone cold.

She smiled soft. "Yeah… You know what?"

Dre raised a brow. "What?"

"I forgot Josiah's bottle at the house. Let me run back real quick — I'll be right back."

Dre's jaw clenched so tight she could see it pulse. "For real?"

Jazmine met his stare dead-on. "Yeah. You know me — I don't move without making sure my baby good."

For a second, she thought he might call her bluff.

Might pull something right there.

But then he gave a sharp little laugh. "Aight. Handle that."

Jazmine smiled — sweet, cool — and stepped out the car like it was nothing.

But the second her feet hit the pavement…

She slid around the corner, heart pounding, and ducked between two crumbling buildings.Pulled out her phone.

First call — Keisha.

Straight to voicemail.

Second call — Keisha again.

Voicemail.

Third call — Tone.

"Yo." His deep voice hit her ear.

"It's Jaz. You know anything about a play on Sistrunk… 15th and 9th? Dre and Keisha sent me."

A pause.

Then Tone's voice dropped cold. "Get the hell off that block. Now."

Her stomach flipped. "What?"

"You ain't hear it from me, but they lining you up. Some dudes waiting inside that house. You

walking into a setup."

Her chest iced over.

"Bet," Jazmine said, her voice flat.

She hung up.

She crouched low in the shadows, watching from two blocks away.

It didn't take long.

Dre sat in the car too long — fidgeting, glancing around.

Then…

Three dudes eased out the side of the duplex, all in dark hoodies, faces half-covered. One with a bat. One with a knife glinting in the streetlight.

One patting something heavy under his hoodie — probably a piece.

They moved like they were waiting for somebody.

Waiting for her.

Jazmine exhaled slow.So that's how it was.

She felt a strange calm settle over her — cold, sharp.

They thought they had her.

Thought she'd fall for it.

But they forgot who they were dealing with.

By the time Dre realized she wasn't coming back, Jazmine was long gone — slipping through side streets like a shadow.

She hit Keisha's block an hour later — hood up, bag tight across her chest.

Her eyes burned with something fierce… something final.

This wasn't over.

Not by a long shot.

They'd tried to line her up like she was a rookie.

But now?

They just made her enemy number one.

And in the streets…

You either a player or a pawn.

Jazmine decided right then — She was done playing small.

Chapter Eight
"Checkmate"

Jazmine didn't move on emotion.

Not anymore.

This wasn't about revenge.

It wasn't even about sending a message.

This was about survival.

About setting the tone.

Because in the streets, if you let one snake bite you and survive…

The rest come slithering.

She hit Tone's shop right after sunrise.

The backroom smelled like fresh fades and stale smoke.

Tone leaned back in a chair, chewing on a toothpick, eyes locked on her like a chess master studying his next move.

"You sure you wanna do this?"

Jazmine nodded once, arms folded. "I'm sure."

Tone gave a slow, approving nod. "Aight. You got backup?"

Jazmine's smirk was sharp as a blade. "I got who I need."

By noon, the word hit the streets — a drop was going down at midnight off Broward. Big play. Big cash.

Jazmine made sure the rumor sounded sweet enough for a snake to bite.
Keisha took the bait.

She texted Dre by 3 PM:

Keisha: This look right. We in.

By 11:30 PM, Jazmine stood in the shadows of the abandoned lot, hoodie drawn low, her heart cold as steel.

Behind her stood two hitters — both masked, both strapped. Quiet soldiers Tone sent.

No questions. No hesitation.

Professional.

At exactly midnight, Keisha's black Civic eased into the lot, headlights cutting through the dark.

Dre rode shotgun — face set, eyes scanning.

They pulled up slow, windows cracked, engine humming like a heart ready to flatline.

Jazmine stepped out the shadows with a calm that felt deadly.

She didn't flinch.

Didn't blink.

Dre's eyes went wide. "Yo… what the hell is this?"

Jazmine said nothing at first — just let the silence drag, thick as the Florida heat.

Keisha cracked a smile, stepping out the car like this was some big joke.

"Jaz, girl… What you doing? We supposed to be family."

Jazmine walked forward, slow and measured. "Family?"

She tilted her head, eyes locking dead on Keisha's.

"You set me up for a robbery with dudes I don't even know. Sent me to a fake drop like I was sweet. And you wanna talk family?"

Keisha's grin slipped.

Dre shifted, hand twitching near his waistband.

One of the masked men behind Jazmine lifted his jacket — chrome flashing in the streetlight.

Dre froze.

Jazmine closed the distance between her and Keisha until they were chest to chest.

"I could have you both laid out right here. No warning. No conversation."

Keisha swallowed hard but kept her chin up. "It wasn't like that."

Jazmine gave a slow, sharp smile. "Then what was it?"

Keisha's silence was loud enough to make the night hum.

Jazmine leaned in, her voice dropping low.

"I don't forget. And I don't forgive."

She stared Keisha down until the older girl dropped her eyes — the first time Jazmine ever saw her blink.

Jazmine stepped back, looking between both of them.

"This your only pass. You cross me again? Ain't no talking. Ain't no warnings. It'll be your name the streets whisper about in the past tense."

She turned, walking away with the same deadly calm she walked in with — her hitters flanking behind her, silent as shadows.

She didn't look back. Didn't have to.

Because when you move like a boss…

You leave people stuck staring at your back, wondering how they played themselves.

That night, the streets changed her name.

Jazmine wasn't just a runner.

She was a problem.

A player who moved with her head on straight and her circle tight. And the game? It had just been flipped in her favor.

Chapter Nine
"The Shift"

The streets talked fast.

By sunrise, word had spread across Fort Lauderdale.

"Jazmine lined Keisha and Dre up… and let 'em walk."

Some called her stupid.

Others called her crazy.

But most?

They called her smart.

Because in a world where everybody's quick to pull a trigger…

The one who moves with strategy?

That's the one you don't cross.

Keisha fell back.

She moved like Jazmine didn't exist — eyes darting away anytime they crossed paths, fake smiles plastered on her face in the rare moments she couldn't avoid her.

Dre?

He played it cool on the surface… but Jazmine felt his eyes every time she stepped in a room.

Snake energy.

Coward energy.

But energy she wasn't pressed about.

Because Jazmine wasn't thinking about Keisha… or Dre.

She was thinking about her next move.

It started small.

A favor here.

A connect there.

She linked with Tone's people — real movers, older cats who respected her grind, not just her face.

She handled low-level plays with precision.

Moved quiet.

Stacked steady.

Never flashy.

Never loud.

But always known.

By the end of the month, she wasn't just making drops.

She was making deals.

Setting her own plays.

Moving weight her way.

She kept her circle tighter than a drum.

Two people in, nobody else.

Trina — a single mom like her, hungry for a way out but loyal to the bone.

Glo — a sharp, quiet girl from the Westside who handled business like a ghost in the wind.

No extras.

No friends.

No snakes.

And with every move, Jazmine felt it.

The shift.

People started greeting her different — nods of respect, words held with care.

Her name started ringing not as Keisha's girl…

But as Jazmine.

On her own.

Late one night, as she stood outside a corner store on Sunrise, Trina looked at her and shook her head, smiling slow.

"You really flipped this whole game, girl."

Jazmine lit a square, exhaled slow, eyes watching the streets move in front of her.

"I ain't even started yet."

But deep down, she knew…

The higher you climb…

The harder the fall when somebody comes for your spot.

And somebody would come.

It was just a matter of when.

Chapter Ten
"New Enemies, Old Rules"

The streets don't forget.

And they don't forgive.Jazmine had stepped into a new world — one where respect was earned in blood and silence, not just money.

Her name was whispered in corners, echoed in club shadows, and eyed suspiciously from rival blocks.

Every move she made rippled like a stone skipping over still water — causing waves she couldn't always control.

The warning signs came subtle at first.

A quick glare from a Westside crew boss at the gas station.

A car that slowed as she walked by on Sunrise Boulevard.

Phones lighting up with texts she didn't recognize.

Then the word hit her through Trina, whispered like a curse:

"They want a cut. Half. Or your head."

Jazmine's chest tightened. Half. Or death.

This wasn't just business.

It was a declaration of war.

Keisha's silence sliced deeper than any insult.

Once her closest ally, now a ghost lurking in the background, her absence a constant reminder of past betrayals.

Dre?

He moved like a shadow in the night — his voice a hiss in dark corners, threats dripping like poison.

But Jazmine wasn't the girl who got set up anymore.

She was the woman who set traps.

That night, Jazmine met Trina and Glo in the back room of an old barbershop — the kind of place where deals are made with nods and eyes, not contracts.

The air was thick with smoke and tension.

"This ain't just about money," Glo said, voice low and fierce. "It's about respect. They wanna make an example."

Jazmine nodded, fists clenched on the table. "Then we better be ready to show them what happens when you cross us."

Trina's eyes burned with a fire that mirrored Jazmine's own. "This time, we ain't playing."But Jazmine felt the weight.

The pressure wasn't just outside.

It pressed in on her at night — when Josiah's breathing slowed, when the world quieted.

Doubt whispered its venomous lies.

Can you really do this?

Can you protect him?

What if you fall?

She swallowed the fear.

Because failure wasn't an option.

The streets are a ruthless chess game.

Every move calculated.

Every ally watched.

Every enemy ready.

Jazmine had to stay three steps ahead — or get taken down.

One week later, a trap sprung.

Jazmine's crew was running a play — low profile, clean, designed to test the rival's reach.

But halfway through, Glo's phone buzzed — a message from an unknown number:

"You're on our turf now. Back off or get handled."

Jazmine's phone buzzed moments later:

"We know where you at."

The warning was clear.

The game was real.

Jazmine gathered her crew — the air thick with adrenaline and unspoken fear.

"We got eyes everywhere. They're watching."

Trina cracked her knuckles. "Let 'em watch. We ain't scared."

Jazmine looked at Glo — her fiercest soldier — and nodded.

"We move smart. We move hard. And we don't give them the satisfaction."

That night, Jazmine sat alone in her apartment — Josiah asleep in the next room.

Her hands trembled for a moment before she clenched them into fists.

This was bigger than her now.

This was survival.

This was legacy.

And no matter what came next…

Jazmine was ready.

Chapter Eleven
"Blood on the Asphalt"

The night was thick with heat and tension, every sound amplified in the humid air.

Jazmine stood with Trina and Glo at the corner of a cracked intersection, the glow of a flickering streetlamp casting long shadows on the cracked pavement.

They weren't just waiting.

They were hunting.

The rival crew's message wasn't empty talk.

They came with numbers, weapons, and rage — ready to take what Jazmine had earned.

Her heart hammered, but her hands stayed steady on the strap of her bag — inside, a cold steel reminder of what she was willing to do.

The first sign was the screech of tires — black SUVs rolling slow down the block.

Windows down, faces hidden in shadows.Dre's voice crackled through a burner phone, cold and sharp.

"This your last warning, Jazmine. Step off or get buried."

Jazmine's eyes narrowed.

She raised the phone, her voice a blade.

"Come get me."

The SUVs stopped. Doors swung open.

Men spilled out — guns glinting under the streetlight, faces hardened and eyes wild.

The air exploded with gunfire.

Jazmine ducked behind a rusted mailbox, her pulse a metronome of survival.

She pulled her piece from her bag — fingers steady despite the chaos — and fired back.

Bullets ripped the night, ricocheting off cracked walls and shattered glass.

Trina and Glo flanked her, moving like shadows, covering every angle.

The world narrowed to breath and gunpowder.

Jazmine's mind was clear — every shot calculated, every move precise.

She wasn't just fighting for her life.

She was fighting for Josiah.

For the woman she was becoming.

A figure lunged from the left — a thug with a jagged knife.

Jazmine sidestepped, grabbing his wrist and twisting it hard until he dropped the blade.

Without hesitation, she swung her fist, catching him square in the jaw.

He stumbled back, dazed — and Jazmine's cold stare told him the fight wasn't over.

Gunfire paused.

Men hesitated, caught off guard by her ferocity.

Then the shooting started again — louder, closer, more desperate.But Jazmine and her crew held the line.

Piece by piece.

Step by step.

Minutes felt like hours.

When the dust finally settled, Jazmine stood breathing hard, heart pounding, eyes scanning.

The street was silent except for the distant wail of sirens.

Bodies lay sprawled — some rivals, some her own.

But Jazmine was still standing.

Still fighting.

Still alive.

Trina dropped to her knees beside Jazmine, wiping sweat and blood from her face.

"We did it," she gasped.

Jazmine nodded, voice hoarse but steady. "Yeah. For now."

Her gaze drifted toward the darkened windows of nearby buildings.

The war wasn't over.

It was only just begun.

Chapter Twelve
"Fallout"

The sirens wailed louder, slicing through the Florida night like a warning shot.

Jazmine wiped the sweat and blood from her brow, standing over a rival laid out on the pavement — chest rising shallow, eyes glassy with shock.

One of hers.

One of theirs.

Didn't even matter anymore.

Because on this side of the game…

Everybody bled the same.

Trina clutched her shoulder, blood seeping through her hoodie, face pale but fierce.

"I'm good," she gritted.

Jazmine gave her a quick once-over. "You sure?"

Trina nodded. "Ain't nothing. I've been shot before."

Jazmine smirked. "Welcome to the family."

Glo came up beside them, pistol still in hand, eyes scanning the shadows.

"We gotta move. Cops gon' sweep this block."

Jazmine glanced around — their car was two blocks down, stashed behind a liquor store.

She grabbed Trina's good arm. "Come on."

They ducked through alleyways slick with sweat, blood, and the heat of gunpowder still hanging in the air.

By the time they hit the car, Jazmine's adrenaline was crashing, her hands shaking for the first time all night.

Not from fear.

From knowing this was only round one.

They sped off into the night, city lights blurring past.

Jazmine kept her eyes straight ahead, jaw clenched.

She wasn't running.

She was regrouping.

By dawn, they holed up at a trap house on the Northside — a low-key spot Tone had blessed her with.

Safe.

For now.

Trina lay on the couch, Glo cleaning her wound with a shaky hand.Jazmine sat on the floor, back against the wall, heart thudding in her ears.

This wasn't a game no more.

This wasn't a hustle.

This was war.

Her phone buzzed.

Tone.

She picked up, voice low. "Yeah?"

"You held your own," Tone said, voice like gravel. "You got the streets talking."

Jazmine exhaled slow. "Let 'em talk."

Tone gave a dark chuckle. "You know what this means, right?"

"Yeah," Jazmine said, her voice cold and even. "I'm in it now. All the way."

She hung up and sat in the silence of the room — her crew battered but alive, the city outside holding its breath.

She knew what was coming.

The rivals would regroup.

The cops would come knocking.

The streets would want a winner.

And Jazmine wasn't about to lose.

She picked up her gun, ran her fingers along the grip.

This wasn't about proving herself anymore.

This was about survival.

About Josiah.

About legacy.

And if she had to get her hands bloody to make that happen?

So be it.

Chapter Thirteen
"The Crown"

The city woke up buzzing.

By noon, every corner from Sistrunk to Sunrise was humming with one name —

Jazmine.

The girl they thought would fold.

The girl they tried to set up.

The girl they came for… and couldn't take down.

Now?

She was the girl running the block.

Tone hit her line early.

"Doors opening. You ready?"

Jazmine sat on the edge of the motel bed, cleaning her piece, voice cool.

"Been ready."

Tone's chuckle came through the line. "Aight then. Move like a queen, Jaz. And don't forget — heavy is the head."

She hung up, staring at her reflection in the cracked mirror.

The crown wasn't given.

It was taken.

And now?

It was hers.

By sundown, Jazmine was back on the Southside, flanked by Glo and Trina, walking straight into the lion's den — the strip the rival crew once controlled.

Heads turned.

Conversations stopped.Eyes wide, whispers low.

Jazmine didn't flinch.

Didn't blink.

She walked the block like she owned it — because now, she did.

The rival crew leader, Ant, stepped out from a corner store, arms folded, two hitters at his back.

"You bold, huh?" Ant said, a slow smirk playing on his lips.

Jazmine met his gaze, cold and sharp. "Bold enough to be standing here while your boys laid out last night."

Ant's grin slipped. "You got heart, lil mama."

Jazmine stepped closer, voice low and laced with steel. "I got more than that. I got soldiers. I got respect. And I got the streets on my side now."

She leaned in, eyes narrowing.

"So… you either fall in line. Or fall off."

The block held its breath.

Ant stared at her for a long, silent second.

Then gave a low, dry laugh.

"Aight. Bet. Respect."

He stuck out his hand.

Jazmine didn't hesitate.

She shook it — firm, strong, unblinking.

When she turned and walked off, the streets buzzed louder than ever.

Jazmine wasn't just a name anymore.

She was the name.

That night, back at the trap house, Trina shook her head, watching Jazmine count a fresh stack.

"You really did it, girl."

Jazmine smirked, stacking the bills. "We did it."Glo leaned back, arms crossed. "Ain't nobody touching us now."

Jazmine's eyes darkened.

"Let 'em try."

But deep down… she knew.

This was just the beginning.

Holding the crown was one thing.

Keeping it?

That's where the real war starts.

Chapter Fourteen
"Enemies in the Shadows"

The streets stayed quiet…

Too quiet.

For two weeks, there were no shots, no threats, no drama.

Jazmine moved weight, stacked bread, and played her role as queen of the block.

People nodded when she passed.

Crew bosses showed respect.

Even Ant fell in line — at least on the surface.

But the streets?

They don't stay loyal for long.

It started with whispers.

Glo mentioned it first.

"Somebody talking."

Jazmine raised a brow. "Talking how?"

Glo shrugged, voice low. "Cops moving weird. Plays getting hit before they drop. Like somebody tipping them off."

Jazmine's heart tightened — instinct kicking in before logic caught up. Somebody close.

Somebody inside.

The next hit came faster.

A drop on Broward got raided.

Two of Jazmine's soldiers locked up.

And when Trina came back from a late-night run, eyes wide, voice shaking, Jazmine knew the walls were closing in.

"I heard your name on a wire, Jaz."

Jazmine blinked. "From who?"

Trina swallowed. "From Dre."

Her blood iced over.

Dre.

The snake that never left the grass.

But it wasn't just him.

"He's got somebody inside," Trina whispered. "He's paying 'em… somebody on your side."

Jazmine's chest burned — hot and cold all at once.

Somebody she trusted.

Somebody she fed.

Somebody who smiled in her face… and sold her out.

That night, she sat in the trap house, gun on the table, staring at her circle.

Trina.

Glo.

Three other soldiers — quiet, loyal… or so she thought.

Her eyes swept over each face.

"We got a rat in the house," she said, her voice low, steady. "And I'm giving y'all one chance."

Silence.Not a twitch.

Not a blink.

Jazmine leaned forward, tapping the barrel of her gun against the wood.

"You better speak now. Or bleed later."

Glo met her eyes — hard, loyal, unshaken.

Trina looked down, fists clenched.

But one of the soldiers…

Reese — the quiet one, the new one — shifted just a little too much.

Jazmine caught it.

Locked eyes with him.

"Something you wanna say, Reese?"

His face cracked — just for a second.

And that's all it took.

Before he could move, Glo snatched him up, slamming him against the wall.

Jazmine stood slow, heart thudding like a war drum.

"You working for Dre?"

Reese shook his head, panic creeping in. "Nah, Jaz… It ain't even like that!"

Jazmine walked up close — too close.

"You feeding him my moves? My drops? You letting him know where I sleep?"

Reese's breath hitched. "Jaz, please…"

Jazmine raised her gun, pressing it under his chin.

"This ain't no game, Reese. And I don't beg for respect."

Silence.

Heavy.

Then… Reese broke."Aight! Aight! He paid me to tip him off! Said you was getting too big… that you was gon' fall anyway!"

Jazmine stared him down, her jaw tight.

"I'm still standing."

She clicked off the safety.

Glo shifted beside her. "What you wanna do?"

Jazmine didn't blink.

She didn't hesitate.

"You know the rules," she said coldly.

Loyalty or death.

The gunshot echoed through the trap house.

Final.

Cold.

Loud enough for the streets to hear.

Jazmine stood over Reese's body, exhaling slow, her heart cold as ice.

She turned to the rest of her crew.

"Anybody else?"

No one moved.

No one spoke.

Because in the game?

The only way to hold a crown…

Is to remind them why you wear it.

Chapter Fifteen
"All In"

The night cracked open with gunfire.

Bullets screamed through the trap house walls — glass exploded, wood splintered, the air thick with smoke and sweat.

Jazmine crouched behind the overturned couch, heart slamming against her ribs, breathing sharp and focused.

Glo fired back from the side door — muzzle flashes lighting her face like war paint.

Trina screamed from the back, "They're coming from both sides!" Jazmine felt it then — not fear… but clarity.

This wasn't just a hit.

This was Dre coming for everything.

And he wasn't alone.

A grenade — small, black, metal — clattered through the front window. Jazmine's eyes went wide.

"MOVE!"

She lunged, grabbing Trina by the arm, dragging her toward the back room as the explosion ripped through the front of the house.

The walls shook.

The air choked with smoke and dust.

Her ears rang, head spinning — but she held on.

Through the haze, shadows moved in — Dre's soldiers, masked, gunned up, ruthless.

Jazmine fired blind — two shots, quick, sharp — dropping one before he hit the floor.

Glo screamed out, "They inside!"

Jazmine spun, heart racing, adrenaline burning hot through her veins.

One of Dre's boys grabbed Trina — yanking her back, gun to her head.

"Drop it!" the man barked at Jazmine.Her mind spun.

Gun pointed.

Trina frozen.

Jazmine's heart slammed against her ribs.

Then Glo slid in from the shadows, her blade flashing clean across the man's throat.

He dropped, choking on blood.

Trina fell to the floor, gasping for air.

Jazmine locked eyes with Glo — both breathing hard, both wide-eyed.

"Good looking," Jazmine whispered.

Glo nodded once. "Ain't done yet."

But they barely had a second.

Because Dre walked in then — slow, deliberate, pistol aimed dead at Jazmine's chest.

"You really thought you was gon' win this?" he sneered.

Jazmine straightened, gun raised, finger tight on the trigger.

"I don't think," she said low. "I move."

They fired at the same time.

Pain ripped through Jazmine's side — white-hot, burning sharp.

Her body jerked, knees nearly buckling.

But Dre dropped too — a bullet tearing through his thigh, sending him crashing into the wall with a shout.

Jazmine clutched her side, blood soaking through her hoodie, but she stayed standing.

Glo ran to her, eyes wild. "Jaz!"

Jazmine gritted her teeth. "I'm good. Handle him."

Dre crawled toward his gun, dragging his leg.

Jazmine stepped over him — pain blazing through her body — and kicked the gun out of his reach.She aimed down, eyes hard as steel.

"You came for me with a whole army… and you still lost."

Dre spat blood, glaring. "This ain't over."

Jazmine cocked her gun.

"No… this is just beginning."

But instead of pulling the trigger…

She pistol-whipped him — hard, fast, sharp across the face.

He dropped — out cold.

Police sirens echoed, closer now.

Trina staggered to her feet.

Glo grabbed Jazmine's arm, trying to steady her.

"We gotta go. Now."

Jazmine's knees threatened to give, but she stood tall.

"I'm walking out. On my feet."

They slipped through the back alley, blood trailing behind Jazmine, heart thudding with every painful step.

She made it to the car — Glo driving, Trina in the back, Jazmine pressing hard against her bleeding side.

As they pulled off into the dark, Jazmine stared at the city rolling past — sirens, flashing lights, the echoes of war still ringing in her ears.

She whispered to herself, voice sharp like a knife:

"If this the price for the crown… I'll pay it every time."

Chapter Sixteen
"The Death of Dre" (Full Expansion)

Dre came to, groggy and bleeding, tied to a steel chair in the center of a dark, concrete basement.

The air stank of mildew, sweat, and something worse — fear.

A single bulb swung overhead, casting shadows on the cracked floor.

And in front of him…

Jazmine.

Arms crossed. Face blank. Eyes cold as stone.

He coughed, choking on his own blood, giving a shaky laugh.

"So this it, huh? You finally caught me slippin'."

Jazmine didn't say a word.

She watched him — silent, unmoved — as Glo circled behind, arms folded, a blade glinting in her hand.

Trina leaned in the doorway, eyes hard, watching every second.

Dre shifted in the chair, his bravado crumbling at the edges.

"You know how this goes, Jaz… it's business. You can't hold it against me."

Her voice dropped — soft, deadly.

"You came for my family. You set me up. You put guns on my people."

She took a slow step forward.

"That ain't business. That's personal."

Dre swallowed hard. His eyes darted between her and the gun at her waist.

"You… you kill me, you gonna have a war on your head."

Jazmine stared at him, face unreadable.

"I already got a war on my head."

She leaned in close — so close he could feel her breath on his skin.

"This… is just me cleaning house."Dre shook his head, voice cracking.

"I got people. You take me out, they coming for you… they coming for that lil' boy of yours—"

Crack.
Jazmine backhanded him — sharp, hard, snapping his head to the side.

"Don't speak on my son."

Her voice was ice.

Blood trickled from the corner of Dre's mouth.

He chuckled, a hollow sound. "You ain't built for this, Jaz…"

Jazmine pulled her pistol slow, unsnapped the safety, and pressed the cold barrel under his chin.

"I was built by this."

For a second, Dre's eyes flickered — panic, regret, something like fear.

But Jazmine didn't blink.

"You lived dirty. You died dirty."

She pulled the trigger.

The shot echoed sharp in the basement, loud and final.

Dre's head snapped back — his body slumped in the chair, lifeless.

Silence fell.

Thick. Heavy. Real.

Jazmine stood there, staring down at the man who once controlled half the city… now just another dead body.

She turned to Glo and Trina.

"Bag him. Make sure the streets find him in the morning."

Trina nodded, face tight. "What you want us to say?"

Jazmine gave a slow, dark smile.

"Don't say nothing. Let them guess."

As she stepped into the night, blood still on her hands, Jazmine felt the weight of everything she'd built — and everything she'd destroyed.

The war with Dre was over.

But the war for the city?

Just getting started.

And Jazmine was ready for every single bullet.

Chapter Seventeen
"Heavy Lies the Crown"

Dre's body hit the streets before sunrise.

Found in an alley off Sunrise and 6th — mouth open, eyes frozen, a clean shot through the head.

Word spread before the police even taped off the scene.

Jazmine did it.

No question.

No witnesses.

No mercy.

By noon, the streets buzzed louder than ever.

Some called her savage.

Some called her stupid.

Most called her queen.

But all eyes were on her now.

At the trap house, Glo scrolled through her phone — news clips, street blogs, fake accounts tagging Jazmine in cryptic posts.

"Dre's people ain't said a word," she said. "But they moving."

Jazmine leaned against the kitchen counter, arms crossed, eyes locked on the silent TV screen flashing Dre's mugshot.

"I don't want words," Jazmine said. "I want them scared to speak my name."

Trina slammed her fist on the table. "They gon' come for us, Jaz. You know that, right?"

Jazmine met her eyes — cool, steady.

"Let 'em."

But deep down…

Jazmine felt it.

The crown was heavy.

And now?

She was wearing it in plain sight.

The first real blow came that night.

A safe house on the Westside — one of hers — got hit.

Doors kicked in. Product gone. Two soldiers left for dead.

No warning.

No name.

Just blood.

Jazmine drove out herself — Glo riding shotgun, Trina in the back.

They rolled up slow — the bodies still lying in the dirt, police nowhere in sight.

Jazmine got out, the Florida air thick and wet with the smell of gunpowder and iron.

One of the dead was Lil Smoke — seventeen, loyal, fresh in the game. Jazmine crouched beside him, jaw tight.

"Damn."

Glo watched her, voice low. "This what comes with it, Jaz. You took out Dre… now they testing you."

Jazmine stood, eyes hard. "Let 'em test me."

She looked around — the neighbors watching from porches, eyes darting away when she caught them staring.

"I'm done playing defense.

"That night, Jazmine called every soldier she had — every block, every corner.

She made one thing clear:

If they ride with her… they ride hard.

If they cross her… they get buried.

The next day, the game changed.

Jazmine started moving heavier, smarter.

She took over Dre's corners.

Cut new deals.

Snatched his alliances out from under him — one by one.

And if anybody whispered otherwise?

She reminded them why Dre wasn't breathing.

But every crown comes with a price.

And Jazmine felt it heavy in her chest…

When she looked at Josiah sleeping.

When she felt the silence of her phone at night.

When she wondered if she could ever walk away from this life.

For now?

She didn't have the luxury of wondering.

For now? She had a city to run.

Chapter Eighteen
"Family Ties"

Jazmine was wide awake when the phone rang.

She'd been sitting on the edge of the bed, staring at her gun on the nightstand — thinking about Dre, about the blood, about everything she lost and everything she was about to lose.

When the screen lit up with "Unknown Caller," she almost let it ring out.

But something in her gut…

She answered.

"Yeah."

A pause.

Then a voice she hadn't heard in months.

"Jazmine… baby… it's Ma."

Jazmine sat back slow, heart tightening.

The last time she heard her mother's voice?

That cold December night — when she told Jazmine to "get her fast ass out my house."

Now?

Now she was calling.

Of course she was.

Her mom cleared her throat. "I… I ain't wanna bother you. I know you busy, and… we don't talk much."
Jazmine didn't say a word.

"I just… I'm behind on my rent. The lights… they fixin' to cut 'em off. And the gas too. I was wonderin'… if you could help."

Jazmine bit her lip until she tasted blood.

She felt her heart folding in on itself — tight, sharp, choking.

This woman… the same one who called her a disappointment, who never showed up for her, who turned her back when Jazmine was fifteen, pregnant, and scared…

Now she needed her.

Jazmine let the silence stretch.

Her mother spoke again — voice soft, like it had weight.

"I wouldn't ask if it wasn't bad… I just… I didn't know who else to call."

That part hit.

Didn't know who else to call.

Same as everybody else.

The crew.

The soldiers.

The family.

Jazmine was everybody's last call — the one they hit when they were desperate.

But when she needed somebody?

Nobody.

Jazmine's voice came out low. "I'll send it.

"Her mother exhaled, rushing with relief. "Thank you, baby. You always been—"

Click.

Jazmine ended the call.

She sat there, staring at the silent phone in her hand.

Not a "How are you?"

Not a "I'm proud of you."

Not a damn "I'm sorry."

Just… need.

Glo came in, saw her sitting there.

"You good?"

Jazmine gave a tight nod. "Yeah."

Glo looked at the untouched food on the table. "Family?"

Jazmine smirked, bitter and cold.

"Yeah. Family."

Glo shook her head, sitting on the arm of the couch.

"Ain't it crazy? You there for everybody… but when you fall? Ain't nobody there for you."

Jazmine looked away, swallowing hard.

"That's why I don't fall."

She wired the money before sunrise.

Didn't call back.

Didn't ask questions.

Because that's what Jazmine did — she showed up for people... even when nobody showed up for her.

And that's exactly why nobody could ever break her.

Because when all she had was herself?

That's when she was the strongest.

Chapter Nineteen
"No Love Lost"

The call came in just after noon.

Glo's voice tight, clipped.

"Yo… you ain't gon' like this."

Jazmine was sitting in her car, parked on Sistrunk, watching a drop go down.

"What?"

Glo hesitated.

"It's… your cousin. Mike."

Jazmine's grip on the steering wheel tightened.

Mike.

Mama's sister's boy.

Family.

The same one she paid rent for last month when his girl kicked him out.

The same one she gave a spot on her crew, just so he could "get his money up."

Now?

"He been talkin'," Glo said flat. "Real reckless. Told a dude from the East that you soft... that you only runnin' 'cause Dre dead."

Jazmine's jaw locked.

"And?"

Glo's voice dropped.

"He tried to move one of your packs. On his own."

Jazmine closed her eyes — fighting the wave that rose in her chest.

It wasn't even about the product.

It wasn't about the streets.

It was about respect.

And family? They supposed to know better.

By sundown, Mike was tied to a chair in the same basement Dre died in.

Some lessons needed to be taught in the dark.

Jazmine walked in slow — Glo standing off to the side, arms folded.

Mike lifted his head, face pale, sweat dripping.

"Jaz... c'mon, it ain't even that serious..."

Jazmine stared him down. "You family, right?"

Mike nodded fast. "Yeah! You know it!"

Jazmine took a slow step forward.

"And what does family not do?"

Mike swallowed hard. "We don't cross each other."

Jazmine smiled — sharp, deadly. "Exactly."

She snatched the gun off the table — flipped it in her hand, metal cold against her palm.

"I gave you a chance. Put money in your pocket. Put food in your kid's mouth."

She leaned in close. "And you played me."

Mike's voice cracked. "It wasn't like that, Jaz. I was just—"

Jazmine slammed the gun down on the table beside him — loud enough to make him jump.

"You was just what?"Mike stuttered. "Tryna... tryna make somethin' shake."

Jazmine's eyes went ice cold.

"I'm the one who makes things shake."

The room went silent. Glo didn't say a word.

Mike stared at the gun — chest heaving.

Jazmine took a deep breath.

Then slid the gun back into her waistband.

"I ain't gon' kill you, Mike."

His shoulders sagged. "Thank you—"

"But you dead to me."

Mike looked up, eyes wide.

"Jaz—"

She turned her back on him. To her?

That was worse than a bullet.

Glo followed her out, footsteps soft.

"You really lettin' him walk?"

Jazmine nodded once.

"Yeah. Let him explain to the streets how he crossed me… and lived."

Glo smirked. "You savage."

Jazmine lit a cigarette, blowing smoke into the thick night air.

"Yeah… but I'm done being stupid."

Chapter Twenty
"The Streets Keep Score"

By morning, word was everywhere.

Mike crossed Jazmine… and lived.

The streets ate it up.

Some called her soft.

Some said she was slipping.

Others whispered she went cold.

But all of them…

They were talking.

Glo stormed into the trap that afternoon, slamming a bag on the table.

"You see this? They testing us already."

She tossed a burner next to the bag.

One of their lookouts — pistol-whipped on his own block.

No money taken.

No product stolen.

Just a message.

Jazmine sat on the couch, slow and steady.

She rolled her eyes toward Glo, her voice cool.

"That's cute."

Glo frowned. "Jaz, you serious? They think you soft now."

Jazmine leaned forward, her eyes sharp as glass.

"Let 'em think it."

Glo's mouth opened — but Trina stepped in, arms crossed.

"She got a plan."Glo shook her head. "She better... 'cause they thinkin' you all heart and no teeth."

Jazmine gave a slow, cold smile.

"Oh... they gon' see my teeth."

That night, she hit back.

Hard.

Every corner that even breathed Mike's name got cleaned out.

Crews that whispered too loud found their stash spots raided.

By sunrise?

Five rivals out of business.

Two of Mike's little street soldiers in the hospital.

Nobody could trace it back to her.

But everybody knew.

By noon, Mike himself rolled out of the city — hit the highway with his girl and his kid, no goodbye, no warning.

Fort Lauderdale wasn't safe for him no more.

Jazmine never said a word.

She didn't have to.

At the trap, Glo raised her glass.

"Lesson taught."

Jazmine clinked bottles with her — a quiet toast.

"They gon' learn. All of 'em."

Trina nodded. "The streets keep score, Jaz… but right now? You winning."

Jazmine sat back, staring at the city lights outside the window.

Yeah.

She was winning.But every win came with a new enemy.

Every move came with a new risk.

And one day?

The score would come due.

Chapter Twenty-One
"Checkmate"

The sun hadn't even touched the sky when Jazmine called the meet.

A roundtable — every soldier, every lieutenant, every face tied to her name.

Some loyal.

Some shaky.

All of them hungry.

They packed into the back of the old warehouse off Andrews Ave — steel doors locked, guards at every exit.

Jazmine stood at the head of the table, arms crossed, eyes sharp.

She didn't speak right away.

She let the silence work on them.

Made 'em sweat.

When she finally spoke, her voice cut like glass.

"I know y'all heard the whispers."

Heads nodded.

"They saying I'm slipping."

A few looked down, some shifted in their seats.

"They think I'm scared 'cause the law knocking at my door."Jazmine leaned forward, her hands flat on the table.

"I ain't never been scared."

Glo stood at her side — quiet, steady, the muscle behind the words.

Trina flanked the other side — arms folded, eyes locked on every face.

Jazmine's voice dropped lower.

"And now? I'm done playing defense. I'm flipping the board."

She pulled a folder from her bag — thick, filled with names, addresses, supply lines.

"Dre's connect in Miami? I'm taking him."

Murmurs shot around the table.

Jazmine slammed the folder down.

"Anybody got a problem with that... speak now."

Nobody said a word.

Jazmine smirked.

"Good."
She laid out the plan — tight, clean, ruthless.

Miami's connect was soft since Dre's fall. No backing. No army.

Jazmine would move in.

Buy him out... or bleed him out.

Either way?

The supply would be hers.

And the law?

Jazmine had a plug in city records — somebody who could keep her a step ahead of the heat.

For the right price.

By the end of the night, her crew rolled out — ready to hit the streets.

Glo stayed behind, giving Jazmine a look."You sure about this?"

Jazmine lit a cigarette, blowing smoke slow.

"If I sit still, they kill me."

She looked Glo dead in the eye.

"This ain't survival. This is war."

As she stepped out into the night, the city humming under her feet...

Jazmine knew one thing.

She wasn't waiting for the streets or the law to make a move.

She was coming for both.

Chapter Twenty-Two
"Miami Heat"

Miami moved different.

Fast.

Loud.

Cutthroat.

Jazmine drove down I-95 herself — no entourage, no soldiers.

This wasn't a war party.

This was a message.

Glo had tried to stop her.

"Jaz… this Miami. They don't play the same way we do."

Jazmine just gave her that look.

"That's exactly why I'm going."She pulled up to the warehouse on NW 7th — Dre's old Miami connect's main spot.

Hector Ruiz.

Cuban.

Mid-40s.

Old school.

Only loyal to money.

And right now…

He was sitting on the product Dre left behind.

Product that should be Jazmine's.

Two guards stepped up as she got out the car.

She didn't blink.

"Tell Hector Jazmine Copeland's here to talk business."

The guards looked her up and down — one laughed under his breath.

"You got business in Lauderdale. You don't run nothin' down here."

Jazmine smiled slow.

"I do now."

Five minutes later, she stood across from Hector in the back office — him behind a desk, a cigar burning between his fingers.

He didn't stand.

Didn't smile.

"You got nerve, little girl."

Jazmine met his eyes.

"And you got product that belongs to me."

Hector leaned back, smirking.

"That product belonged to Dre. Dre's dead."

Jazmine's face didn't move.

"Exactly. Which means it's mine."Hector chuckled, shaking his head.

"I don't move for threats, sweetheart."

Jazmine leaned forward — voice like ice.

"This ain't a threat. This is your only chance."

Hector's smile faded.

He studied her — hard, cold, calculating.

Then… he laughed again.

"You got balls… I'll give you that."

He flicked ash into a tray.

"Alright. Fifty percent."

Jazmine tilted her head.

"I'm taking eighty."

Hector barked a laugh.

"You'll be dead before you make it back to Lauderdale."

Jazmine smiled — slow, deadly.

"Then you better make that first shot count."

The room went silent.

Hector stared… then leaned forward slow.

"Eighty. You move my product too. You protect my lines… and I'll protect yours."

Jazmine locked eyes with him.

"Deal."

They shook once.

The deal done.

But neither trusted the other.And that's exactly how Jazmine liked it.

As she walked back to her car, the heat pressing down thick…

Jazmine knew Miami wouldn't fold easy.

But this was her world now.

And she was coming for every piece of it.

Chapter Twenty-Three
"Back to the Block"

By the time Jazmine hit Lauderdale city limits, the streets were already buzzing.

Word travels fast.

Too fast.

She stepped into the trap house on 6th and Sunrise — the spot humming with tension.

Glo was there.

Trina too.

And a few faces she didn't like the look of.

Glo stood when Jazmine walked in.

"Miami called already. Said y'all got a deal."

Jazmine nodded, dropping her keys on the table.

"Eighty percent."

Trina whistled low. "Damn. You ain't come to play."

But it was the look on Glo's face that caught her.

"You got a problem?"

Glo crossed her arms.

"Nah. I'm just wonderin'… you trustin' Miami now?"Jazmine's eyes sharpened.

"I don't trust nobody."

One of the lieutenants — Tone — spoke up from the corner.

"Word is… some of Dre's old boys ain't happy you cutting deals outside the city. They say you moving different. Like you forgetting who fed you first."

Jazmine's head snapped toward him.

"I ain't forget nothin'."

She walked up on Tone, eyes locked.

"But if anybody think I owe 'em something… they can step the hell off my line."

Silence.

Hard. Thick.

Tone nodded — low, tight. "Say less."

Glo gave Jazmine a long look.

"You sure you ain't spreadin' yourself too thin?"

Jazmine smirked.

"I'm spreadin' myself exactly how I want. And anybody can get touched — Miami...

Lauderdale... hell, even family."

Trina gave a half-smile. "Then let's get it."

But even as they set the next move in motion...

Jazmine felt it.

That crack in the armor.

Her people were riding.

But loyalty?

That could flip in a heartbeat.

And the only thing harder than building an empire...Was keeping it.

Chapter Twenty-Four
"Pressure Busts Pipes"

The streets stayed quiet for two days.

Too quiet.

Jazmine moved through the city like a shadow — drops happening, money flipping, Miami deals locking in.

But something… felt off.

Eyes followed her.

Conversations stopped when she walked in.

And Glo?

Glo felt it too.

It broke open on a Thursday night.

Trina stormed into the backroom of the trap, breath tight.

"You ain't gonna believe this—"

Jazmine looked up from the bag she was packing.

"What?"

Trina threw a burner on the table.

"Check the last text."

Jazmine scrolled — her heart punching against her ribs.

It was a message chain between Tone… and a name she knew too well.

Reek.One of Dre's old shooters.

Tone: "She movin light. Miami's got her wide open."

Reek: "Say the word. We'll flip the block."

Tone: "Let me line it up."

Jazmine dropped the phone, her face stone.

Tone — her own soldier.

Setting her up.

Glo walked in right behind Trina, eyes dark.

"What you wanna do?"

Jazmine stood slow, her voice ice.

"Where's Tone now?"

Trina didn't blink. "He's outside. On the block. With two of his boys."

Jazmine grabbed her jacket.

"Let's go teach 'em about pressure."

Fifteen minutes later, Jazmine pulled up on the corner — blacked-out Tahoe, windows down.

Tone stood there, laughing with his boys like nothing was about to happen.

Jazmine stepped out, cool as the breeze, Glo and Trina flanking her.

She walked straight up — no words.

Pistol already in her hand.

Tone barely turned before—

Crack!

Jazmine pistol-whipped him hard — the force dropping him to his knees.

"Thought I was movin' light?" she hissed.

Tone scrambled back, blood on his lip.

"Jaz… it wasn't like that…"

She aimed the gun at his forehead."It was exactly like that."

Glo dragged the other two off to the side — handling them while Trina stood watch.

Jazmine crouched low — face inches from Tone's.

"I give people chances, Tone. I feed 'em. I ride for 'em."

She pressed the barrel to his head.

"And this how you pay me back?"

Tone shook his head, eyes wide. "It was Reek… he said—"

Jazmine cut him off.

"I don't care what Reek said."

Her finger flexed on the trigger.

"But I want you to send him a message."

She stood up, lowered the gun… and shot him.

Once.

In the leg.

Tone screamed, hitting the ground.

Jazmine stood over him, cold.

"You tell Reek… he can come see me himself."

She nodded to Glo and Trina.

"Bag him. Drop him on Reek's block."

Glo smirked. "With pleasure."

Jazmine walked away as Tone's screams echoed into the night.

Her heart beat steady.

Because loyalty?

Was earned in blood.Chapter Twenty-Six — "Hunted"

The streets whispered louder now.

Reek's coming.

Word hit every block by morning.

He wasn't sending shooters.

He wasn't talking behind backs.

Reek said it himself:

He was coming for Jazmine.

Glo slammed her phone on the table.

"He's bold as hell."

Trina loaded her clip, shaking her head.

"He must think you Dre."

Jazmine stood by the window, staring at the street below.

"He think I'm dead."

But what Reek didn't know…

Jazmine wasn't hiding.

She was hunting him.

That night, she set the bait.

One of Reek's boys — a runner named Smoke — got picked up on the Southside.

Jazmine let him go.

On purpose.With a message.

"Tell Reek I'll be at the docks. Midnight."

The city buzzed with it.

By sundown, half the streets were waiting to see if Jazmine showed.

The other half were betting she'd be dead by morning.

But Jazmine didn't flinch.

She rolled up to the docks alone.

No backup.

No crew.

Just her… and a .45 on her hip.

Reek showed up fifteen minutes late — four soldiers behind him.

He stepped out the car grinning, gun tucked at his side.

"Well, well… the queen herself."

Jazmine kept her face blank.

"Cute. You brought a welcome committee."

Reek chuckled.

"Couldn't let you walk outta here, Jaz. You know that."

Jazmine shrugged.

"I know."

Before Reek could blink…

Pop! Pop! Pop!

Three shots cracked through the air.

Reek's soldiers dropped — hit from the shadows.

Glo and Trina stepped out from behind a shipping crate — silencers smoking.

Reek spun back to Jazmine — eyes wide, breath caught.

"You set me up."Jazmine smiled — slow, deadly.

"No… you set yourself up."

She pulled her .45.

"One thing you should've learned, Reek…"

She aimed dead at his chest.

"You don't hunt me."

Bang.

One shot.

Right through the heart.

By the time his body hit the ground, Jazmine was walking back to her car.

Calm.

Steady.

Done.

The streets would talk about this one.

How Reek came hunting… and got hunted.

And Jazmine?

She just tightened her grip on the throne.

Chapter Twenty-Five
"The Price of the Crown"

The victory still tasted fresh — Reek gone, her grip tighter than ever.

But the streets don't forgive.

Not even for queens.It was a quiet night — the kind that never lasts.

Glo was running point on a drop, Jazmine back at the safe house, counting money and planning the next move.

Then the call came.

"Jaz… it's Tone."

Her heart skipped — but she didn't flinch.

"Yeah?"

Glo's voice was sharp, urgent.

"He's hurt bad. Gunshot to the chest. Hospital won't give location."

Jazmine's breath caught.

Tone — the same man she left bleeding in the streets — was bleeding again.

But this time… it was different.

She hit the streets, her mind racing.

Who would shoot Tone?

Enemy crew?

Revenge?

Or… betrayal inside?

At the hospital, the smell of antiseptic and pain hit her like a wave.

Glo met her at the door — face grim.

"No visitors."

Jazmine clenched her fists.

"I'm not leaving."

Hours passed.

Then a doctor stepped out.

"Mr. Tone is stable but critical. He's awake."Jazmine pushed through, heading to the ICU room.

Tone lay there, pale but alive.

His eyes opened — focus sharp despite the tubes.

"Jaz…"

She sat down beside him, voice low.

"Who did this?"

Tone hesitated — then whispered, "It wasn't them…

it was us."

Jazmine's heart sank.

"Who?"

Tone's voice cracked.

"Glo…"

Jazmine's mind spun.

Glo? Her rock?

Her right hand?

It didn't add up.

But in this game?

Trust was a luxury.

And every crown had its shadows.

Chapter Twenty-Six
"Betrayal in the Ranks"

The air was thick in the safe house — tension crawling over every surface like smoke.

Jazmine sat at the head of the table, eyes cold and tired.

Glo stood across from her, face unreadable, hands clenched.

The room held its breath.

"Why, Glo?" Jazmine's voice broke the silence.

Glo didn't flinch.

"It was a choice," she said, voice low but steady.

Jazmine's jaw tightened.

"A choice? You put a bullet in Tone?"

Glo's eyes flickered with something Jazmine couldn't place.

"I did what I had to do."

The room shifted; Trina stepped closer, fists clenched.

"You betrayed us all."

Glo shook her head.

"This ain't personal. This is survival."

Jazmine's gaze pierced through her old friend.

"Survival? Or power?"

Glo met her stare without backing down.

"The streets don't care about loyalty. Only strength."

Jazmine stood, pacing slow, mind racing.

"How long?"

Glo swallowed hard.

"Since the Miami deal."

A cold weight settled in Jazmine's chest.

Every move she made, every deal she closed… Glo was working the other side.

The enemy was closer than she ever imagined.

Jazmine stopped pacing, eyes blazing."This ends tonight."

Chapter Twenty-Seven
"Queen's Justice"

The trap house cleared out fast.

Word got around: Jazmine and Glo were about to handle it… the old way.

Face to face.

One shot.

Winner walks away.

Trina tried to stop it.

"Jaz… this don't gotta go like this."

Jazmine shook her head, eyes locked on Glo.

"It always had to."

Glo stood in the center of the room — gun loose in her hand, shoulders squared.

"You sure about this?" Glo asked, voice calm.

Jazmine stepped forward, gun in hand, safety off.

"I'm done being sure. I'm just ready."

They circled each other — two women who built an empire together... now ready to tear each other apart.

Glo smirked.

"You changed, Jaz."

Jazmine kept her eyes hard.

"No. I woke up."Glo raised her gun first.

Bang.

Jazmine moved — fast, low — the bullet grazing her shoulder.

She hit the ground, rolled, fired back.

Pop.

Glo stumbled — caught in the side.

The room exploded in shouts — but nobody moved.

This was between them.

Glo dropped to one knee, blood soaking her shirt.

Jazmine walked up slow — gun aimed dead center.

Glo looked up, breathing hard.

"I was your sister."

Jazmine's heart slammed in her chest — but her hand didn't shake.

"And you still crossed me."

For a moment... just a moment... it felt like everything they'd been through flashed between them.

The streets.

The hustle.

The war.

All of it.

Then Jazmine pulled the trigger.

Bang.

Glo hit the ground — eyes open, staring at the ceiling.

Trina covered her mouth, tears slipping out.

Jazmine stood over the body — silent, stone.

Because this wasn't about love.This was about loyalty.

The crown was hers now.

But at what cost?

Chapter Twenty-Eight
"The Sit Down"

The warehouse was dead silent when Jazmine walked in.

Every lieutenant.

Every runner.

Every hitter.

They all showed up.

Some came to pay respect.

Some came to test her.

Some… came to watch her fall.

Jazmine stood at the head of the long table, Trina posted at her right side — eyes cold, gun on her hip.

The room shifted, all eyes locked on the woman who just took out her right hand.

Jazmine let the silence ride for a long, thick moment.

Then her voice sliced through the air — low, sharp, unapologetic.

"Glo made her choice."

A few heads nodded.

A few looked down.

Jazmine didn't blink.

"She thought power meant moving behind my back... working against me."

She leaned forward, hands flat on the table."And now she's gone."

One of the younger lieutenants — Rico — cleared his throat.

"Word on the street is... you killed your own."

Jazmine's eyes snapped to him — razor sharp.

"I didn't kill my own. I took out a snake."

The room got real quiet.

Jazmine stepped around the table, pacing slow, her voice never raising.

"If anybody here got questions about where I stand — say it now."

She stopped walking.

"If you think I'm weak?" She pointed to the door. "Leave."

She scanned the room.

"If you think I won't do what I have to?" She tapped her chest. "Test me."

Nobody moved.

Nobody spoke.

Jazmine gave a slow, cold smile.

"Good."

She walked back to the head of the table, grabbed a chair, and sat down.

"Now… we got business to handle. Glo's territory is open. The Miami pipeline is ours. Reek is dead. I need soldiers who are all in — because the next move?"

She locked eyes with every face in the room.

"We taking everything."

One by one, heads nodded.

Some out of fear.

Some out of respect.

But all of them… followed.Trina leaned over, whispering just loud enough for Jazmine to hear.

"You still got 'em."

Jazmine stared straight ahead, voice low.

"For now."

Twenty-Nine
"Enemies in Every Corner"

The first hit came two days after the sit-down.

A stash house on Broward got raided — not by cops…

But by masked hitters nobody recognized.

Product gone.

Two of her runners shot.

Jazmine stood in the wrecked house, staring at the bloodstains on the floorboards.

Trina knelt beside the empty duffel bags.

"Whoever did this… they ain't amateurs."

Jazmine's jaw tightened.

"They're watching us."

The second hit came the next night.

One of her delivery cars — torched in broad daylight outside a corner store on Sunrise.

Message clear.

We're coming.Glo's death made Jazmine queen.

But it also made her vulnerable.

At the trap, Rico slammed a map on the table.

"Look — they hit Northside. They hit Broward. They hit Sunrise. All in forty-eight hours."

He circled the spots with a red marker.

"They're pushing in from every angle."

Jazmine folded her arms, eyes cold.

"And they think I'm gonna fold."

Rico gave her a look — uncertain, but loyal.

"What's the move?"

Jazmine tapped the map with her finger.

"We don't defend."

She leaned forward, her voice like steel.

"We attack."

Trina smirked.

"Who first?"

Jazmine stared at the names on the list — crews creeping into her territory, enemies whispering her name, Miami rivals trying to get a foothold in her city.

"All of them."

Because this wasn't about holding the crown anymore.

The first move came at midnight.

Trina led the Southside hit — sliding through in two dark sedans, silencers ready.

By sunrise, two of the rival crew's stash spots were gone.
No survivors.

No questions.

The second move?

Northside.

Jazmine went herself.

She pulled up to a corner block that used to belong to Glo's cousin, now flipped by a hungry crew from Carol City.

Jazmine stepped out — pistol in hand, mask pulled low.

Three hitters posted on the steps.

They barely had time to blink.

Bang. Bang. Bang.

Jazmine dropped them clean.

By the time the rest of the crew came running out, Glo's old shooters — loyal to Jazmine now — boxed them in from the back.

It wasn't a fight.

It was a slaughter.

By dawn, Northside was silent.

And the word hit the streets fast.

Jazmine wasn't on defense.

She was coming for everything.

At the warehouse later that night, Rico laid out the final map."You cleared every block they hit... and then some."

He looked up, a little awe in his eyes.

"You made 'em run."

Jazmine sat at the head of the table, cleaning her gun slow.

"They'll be back."

Trina nodded. "Then we stay ready."

Jazmine leaned back in her chair — her face calm, but her heart ice cold.

Because this wasn't the end.

This was the beginning.

And if the streets wanted war?

She'd give it to them.

Thirty
"Why I Fight"

The house was quiet.

Not the trap.

Not the warehouse.

Home.

A small, three-bedroom off Sistrunk — nothing flashy.

The only place in this world that felt like hers.

Jazmine sat on the edge of her son's bed, watching him sleep.J.J. — seven years old.

Her heart.

Her reason.

He slept hard, a soft snore slipping from his lips, one little hand tucked under his cheek.

Jazmine reached out, brushing a curl from his forehead.

His skin was warm.

His breath soft.

So small.

So innocent.

She swallowed hard, that knot rising in her chest.

This life… this war… it wasn't supposed to touch him.

She built every move, fought every battle… for him.

So he'd never have to fight like she did.

The streets called her a queen.

The law called her a criminal.

Her family called her a disappointment.

But to him?

She was just Mom.

A little voice broke the silence.

"Mommy?"

Jazmine blinked — his eyes cracked open, sleepy and soft.

"Yeah, baby?"

He reached out — tiny fingers curling around hers.

"You okay?"

Her heart squeezed tight.

She leaned down, kissed his forehead."I'm good, baby."

J.   J. yawned, eyes fluttering.

"You gonna be here tomorrow?"

Jazmine's throat burned.

"Yeah… I'll be here."

He drifted back to sleep, holding her hand like a lifeline.

Jazmine sat there long after his breathing evened out…

Staring at the quiet rise and fall of his chest.

For him…

She'd burn the whole damn world down.

Chapter Thirty-One
"They Came for Me"

It happened at 6:47 AM.

Jazmine was still at home — sipping coffee at the kitchen counter, eyes on the morning news.

K. J. was in his room, getting ready for school.

Just another morning.

Until it wasn't.

BAM! BAM! BAM!

The front door exploded open.

Jazmine dropped the mug — glass shattering.

Men in black masks rushed in, guns raised.She moved on instinct — flipping the table for cover, grabbing the .40 tucked in her waistband.

Shots cracked through the house.

Walls splintered.

Windows shattered.

"J.J.!"

She screamed, heart ripping in half.

Two masked men tried to hit the hallway.

Pop! Pop!

Jazmine dropped both — dead before they hit the floor.

She sprinted toward her son's room, dodging bullets, heart in her throat.

J.   J. stood in the doorway — eyes wide, frozen in fear.

"Get down!"

She tackled him to the floor as bullets ripped into the wall above their heads.

She crawled over him, shielding his body with hers, gun up.

Another mask came into view — shotgun raised.

BANG.

Jazmine fired first — straight through his chest.

He dropped hard.

The house went quiet.

Real quiet.

Jazmine stayed on the floor, holding J.J. tight, her breath ragged.

"You okay, baby?"

K.   J. nodded — eyes wet, but brave.

"Yeah… Mommy, I'm okay."

Her heart slammed inside her chest — rage boiling like fire in her veins.They didn't come for her turf.

They didn't come for her money.

They came for her.

For her family.

This wasn't business.

This was personal.

And whoever sent them?

Jazmine was going to find them.

And bury them.

Chapter Thirty-Two
"Hunt or Be Hunted"

By nightfall, the trap house was packed.

Trina stood to Jazmine's right — eyes blazing.

Rico, Tone (still limping from his last run-in), and half the Northside crew flanked the room.

Guns loaded.

Eyes hard.

Loyalty unspoken… but thick in the air.

Jazmine slammed a photo on the table.

Derrick "D-Roc" Hanes.

Ex-Miami hitter.

Small-time boss.

Known snake.

Word was... he wanted a piece of Broward.

Now?
He was on Jazmine's list.Trina glanced at the photo, lip curling.

"That fool sent shooters to your house?"

Jazmine's face stayed stone.

"They came for my son."

The room went dead silent.

Jazmine looked around — her voice ice cold.

"This ain't about turf. This ain't about power. This is about blood."

She tapped the photo once.

"I want him alive."

She locked eyes with every face in the room.

"So I can take my time."

Rico nodded, sliding a clip into his Glock.

"Say less."

They rolled out thirty deep that night — every block they hit, people backed off.

By midnight, D-Roc's main spot was lit up.

Glo's old connects tipped them off — he was laying low in a motel off 441.

Jazmine walked in first.

Kicked the door open.

D-Roc scrambled — half-dressed, reaching for a gun.

He didn't make it.

Jazmine fired once — through his shoulder.

He hit the floor screaming.

She stepped over him, pistol pressed to his mouth.

"You came for my son?"He shook his head fast, eyes wide with fear.

"I swear… it wasn't me… it was—"

Bang.

She shot him in the other shoulder.

"You sure?"

D-Roc sobbed, coughing blood.

"It was the Cartel… Miami… they said if I didn't hit you, they'd come for me."

Jazmine smiled slow.

"Now I'm coming for them."

She stood, blood on her boots, heart ice cold.

Because this wasn't just war anymore.

This was personal business.

And business was about to get bloody.

Chapter Thirty-Three
"For My Son"

The sun hadn't even come up yet.

Jazmine sat on the edge of her bed, staring at the sleeping figure curled beside her.

J. J.

Breathing soft.

Safe.

For now.

She reached out, brushing her fingers over his small hand — the same hand that clutched hers every night since the attack.

She had moved him out of the house.

Not to family.Not to the hood.

But to a private condo on the beach — rented under a fake name, guarded by two men she trusted with her life.

Jazmine would burn the world before she let it touch him again.

A soft knock tapped against the doorframe.

Trina stepped inside — eyes softer than usual.

"He's good here, Jaz. We'll double the security."

Jazmine nodded, standing slowly.

"I'm done risking him."

Trina gave her a look.

"You done risking yourself?"

Jazmine smirked — a shadow of a smile.

"I'm never done risking myself."

She leaned down, pressed a kiss to J.J.'s forehead.

He stirred, half-asleep, mumbling…

"Mommy… you stayin'?"

Jazmine swallowed the lump in her throat.

"For a little while, baby."

Because after this next move?

She didn't know if she'd make it back.

But if she didn't handle this now…

They'd never stop coming.

Jazmine stood, straightened her jacket, and gave Trina a look.

"Let's finish this."

For her city.For her name.

For her son.

Chapter Thirty-Four
"Cartel Business"

Miami — Brickell Avenue.

Cartel territory.

Gated condos, sleek foreign cars, the kind of money that never saw the hood.

Jazmine rolled up in a matte black Range Rover — windows down, Trina riding shotgun, Rico and Tone in the back.

No masks.

No sneak moves.

She wanted them to see her coming.

The doorman didn't even blink when Jazmine walked into the lobby.

She was expected.

An elevator opened to the penthouse — two men in black suits flanking the doors.

One of them nodded.

"Mr. Morales will see you now."

Jazmine walked in slow, every step a statement.

Hector Morales sat behind a glass desk — Miami Cartel's golden boy. Late thirties.

Cuban.

Always wearing that smug little smirk.He leaned back in his chair, cigar lit, eyes sharp.

"Well, well… the Queen of Lauderdale. Finally decided to stop hiding."

Jazmine stopped a few feet from his desk, hands at her sides, voice flat.

"I'm not hiding. I'm hunting."

Hector laughed — low, slow.

"You killed my runner… torched my spots… and you show up here alone?"

Jazmine tilted her head.

"Who said I'm alone?"

The elevator dinged.

Trina, Rico, and Tone stepped out — guns drawn, dead silent.

Hector's smile faded.

"You got some nerve."

Jazmine leaned forward, eyes like fire.

"You sent men to my house… where my son sleeps."

Her voice dropped to a whisper.

"So now… I'm here for you."

Hector stood, smoothing his jacket.

"You ain't walking outta here."

Jazmine smiled — slow, dangerous.

"You better hope I don't."

For a second… the room went ice cold.

The kind of still before everything explodes.

Because this wasn't business anymore.

This was blood for blood.

Chapter Thirty-Five

"The Penthouse Shootout"

Hector Morales reached for his gun.

Big mistake.

BANG.

Jazmine fired first — the bullet ripping through his shoulder, spinning him into his glass desk.

Glass shattered.

The cigar dropped.

And the whole room exploded.

Trina hit the first bodyguard with a clean headshot.

Pop!

Rico swept the room, firing off at the second — catching him in the chest.

Tone kicked over the desk, spraying lead into the hallway as more Cartel muscle stormed in.

Hector crawled for his gun, blood pouring from his arm.

Jazmine stalked after him, her Glock steady.

"You should've never touched my family."

He spun back, wild eyes, hand reaching—

Pop!

Jazmine shot him in the leg — point-blank.

Hector screamed, collapsing.

The penthouse filled with smoke and gunfire.

Cartel men swarmed the doorway — but Trina and Rico handled them like clockwork.

One dropped.

Another dropped.Tone caught a bullet in the side — grunted, but stayed firing.

Jazmine grabbed Hector by the collar, dragging him across the floor.

"You thought I'd fold?"

She slammed him against the wall.

"You thought you'd scare me?"

She pressed the barrel to his forehead.

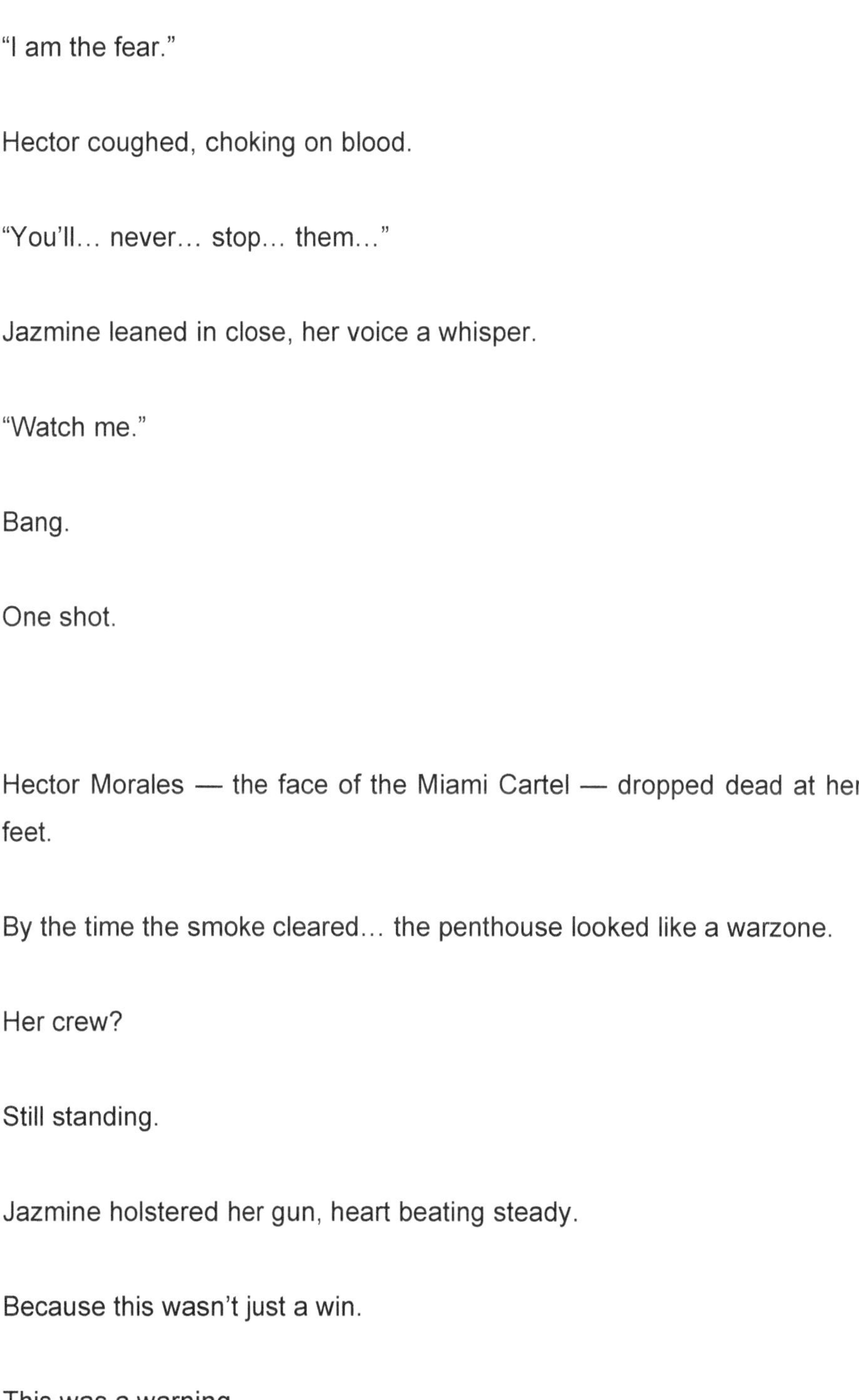

"I am the fear."

Hector coughed, choking on blood.

"You'll… never… stop… them…"

Jazmine leaned in close, her voice a whisper.

"Watch me."

Bang.

One shot.

Hector Morales — the face of the Miami Cartel — dropped dead at her feet.

By the time the smoke cleared… the penthouse looked like a warzone.

Her crew?

Still standing.

Jazmine holstered her gun, heart beating steady.

Because this wasn't just a win.

This was a warning.

The Cartel wasn't untouchable.

Chapter Thirty-Six
"Checkin' on Tone"

The sun was creeping over the horizon when they made it back to the Broward safe house.

Trina was checking the perimeter.

Rico was loading fresh clips, quiet and focused.

Jazmine walked through the living room, wiping dried blood from her knuckles.

Her eyes landed on Tone — slumped on the couch, clutching his side where the bullet grazed him.

He looked up when she stepped in.

"You ain't gotta check on me, Jaz."

Jazmine crossed her arms, leaning against the doorframe.

"I didn't ask."

Tone tried to smirk — but winced, his hand pressing against his ribs.

"Cartel's gonna want blood for this."

Jazmine tilted her head, voice calm.

"They already got it."

Tone shook his head.

"You know this ain't over."

Jazmine walked over, grabbed the med kit off the table, and dropped it on his lap.

"It is for tonight."

Tone stared at her for a long second.

"You ain't gotta patch me up, Jaz."

Jazmine gave him a look — sharp, but real.

"You're my crew."

She opened the kit, kneeling beside him.

"I don't leave mine bleeding."Tone let out a slow breath, leaning back as she cleaned the wound.

For a minute… there was no boss, no soldier… just two people who survived too much.

"You trust me, Jaz?" Tone asked quietly.

Jazmine met his eyes, steady.

"With my life."

Tone swallowed hard.

"Then let me have your back when this Cartel heat hits."

Jazmine gave him a half-smile — small but real.

"You already do."

She finished wrapping his side, stood up, and offered him a hand.

Tone grabbed it — grip tight, solid.

Because in this world?

Loyalty wasn't given.

It was earned in blood.

Chapter Thirty-Seven
"The Weight of It All" (15-Year-Old Flashback)

The backroom stayed dark.

Jazmine sat there alone — the same spot she always landed when the weight got too heavy.

Tonight, it pressed harder than ever.

Her eyes fixed on the half-empty bottle in front of her.

Not the liquor.

Not the gun beside it.But the reflection staring back at her in the dark glass.

A girl who'd been fighting since she was fifteen.

Fifteen.

Baby in her belly.

Mama screaming in her face.

"You out here fast and grown — now what? Ain't nobody coming to save you!"

She remembered standing on that porch with nothing but a trash bag of clothes and a world of shame.

Nowhere to go.

No one to call.

That first pack got placed in her hand by a dude she barely knew — a dealer who didn't give a damn about her age.

"You wanna eat? You better learn how to eat."

She did.

Fast.

The first sale?

Tears in her eyes.

But diapers don't buy themselves.

The first time she saw death up close?

It wasn't a warning.

It was a mirror.

The game didn't give her a choice.

It gave her a reason.

And here she was… years later… queen of a world she never asked for.

Her son's face flashed through her mind.

That smile.Those eyes.

The reason she fought.

The reason she killed.

The reason she kept breathing.

Trina's soft knock broke through the silence.

"You good, Jaz?"

Jazmine wiped at her eyes — blinked hard until her face turned to stone again.

"I'm good."

Because no matter how much this game took…

She refused to let it take her.

Chapter Thirty-Eight
"Miami Sends Its Message"

It came in a box.

Left on the hood of Trina's car outside the trap.

No name.

No note.

Just a plain black shoebox with a red ribbon.

Rico spotted it first.

He picked it up like it was nothing… until he heard something shift inside.

He popped the top.

And what he saw turned his stomach.

A severed hand.

Tatted.Familiar.

Rico cursed under his breath, heart thudding.

It was Benny's — one of their Broward hitters, missing since last week.

Now they knew why.

Trina stormed outside, eyes blazing.

"What the hell is that?"

Rico showed her.

Trina's jaw clenched.

"This Miami's answer."

By the time Jazmine pulled up, the whole crew was tight.

She stepped out, eyes dropping to the box.

She didn't blink.

Didn't flinch.

Didn't say a word.

Trina walked up slow, voice low.

"What's the move?"

Jazmine stared at the hand like it was nothing but trash on the street.

She pulled out her lighter…

And set the box on fire.

She watched it burn, flames licking the sky, smoke curling like a warning shot.

"War."

Her voice was calm.

Ice cold.

"This ain't a message." She turned to her crew. "This is a challenge."

Rico nodded.Trina smirked.

Tone loaded his clip.

Because if Miami wanted war?

They just got it.

Chapter Thirty-Nine
"Crossroads"

It started like nothing.

Jazmine was posted at the gas station on Sunrise — hoodie up, trying to keep low.

Just her, a Black & Mild, and a world of weight on her shoulders.

"Damn… Jazmine Copeland?"

She turned.

And there he was.

Marcus.

Clean cut.

Fitted hat low.

Smile like he never left home.

They went way back — John I. Leonard High.

He used to let her copy homework.

Used to walk her home when dudes got too bold.

Never asked for nothing.

Jazmine blinked, caught off guard.

"Marcus?"

He laughed — that same easy laugh she remembered.

"Didn't think I'd see you on this side of town."They talked.

About nothing…

About everything…

And for the first time in a long time, Jazmine wasn't talking with her guard up.

He wasn't in the game.

Had a legit job.

No dirt.

No secrets.

When he smiled at her, it wasn't like the dudes on the block.

It wasn't fear.

It wasn't respect.

It was… real.

And for a second, she let herself wonder…

Could there be more for her?

Could she leave this behind?

They exchanged numbers.

Marcus hugged her before he left — strong, warm, nothing extra.

"Be safe, Jaz."

She felt it.

All of it.

As he pulled off…

Jazmine stood there for a long moment, heart thudding.

The streets gave her power.

But could love give her peace?

Chapter Forty
"Heat Rising"

The night air was thick with smoke and tension.

Broward streets burned — tires slashed, corners flipped, runners disappearing into the shadows.

Jazmine's crew moved fast — but Miami's Cartel hit back harder.

Explosions in safe houses.

Shots fired in broad daylight.

And whispers on every block: the Queen of Lauderdale was about to fall.

At the trap house, Jazmine paced — gun in hand, nerves fraying.

Trina was on the phone, arranging back-up.

Rico cleaned his piece, jaw tight.

Tone leaned against the wall, eye twitching.

"Everybody ready?" Jazmine asked — voice cold but steady.

A nod all around.

The call came just as they were gearing up.

Her phone lit up — Marcus.

She hesitated.

"Jaz," his voice was calm, steady.

"I know it's crazy out there. Just… be careful."

Her heart thumped — more than the gunfire outside.

"I'm here. Anytime you wanna talk… or get out."

Jazmine stared at the screen — a flicker of hope cutting through the chaos.

But the streets?

They didn't wait for hope. They only knew war.

She tucked the phone away, eyes hardening.

"Let's show Miami what happens when you push too far."

Because no matter how loud the heat got…

Jazmine wasn't backing down.

Not now.

Not ever.

Chapter Forty-One

"All In"

The night was electric — every corner crackling with tension, every shadow a potential enemy.

Jazmine stood at the front of her crew, eyes blazing with a fire that didn't quit.

"This is it," she said, voice steady but fierce.

"We either take 'em down tonight… or we don't come back."

Trina loaded her gun, smirking.

"Queen don't back down."

Rico nodded, checking his ammo.

Tone cracked his neck — pain forgotten in the rush.

They moved like a storm — swift, brutal, unstoppable.Every safe house hit.

Every stash destroyed.

Every threat eliminated.

Gunfire echoed through the night like thunder.

Shots rang out — some close, some far.

Jazmine was everywhere — leading, killing, surviving.

Hours later, as the smoke cleared and the sun crept up…

The Cartel's grip was shattered.

But the cost?

It was written in the silence of her crew — the missing, the wounded, the broken.

Jazmine stood alone on the rooftop, breathing hard.

The city spread out below — bruised, battered… but still hers.

She pulled out her phone.

Marcus's name flashed.

She answered.

"Did you make it through?"

His voice was steady, warm.

"I did."

For the first time in a long time… Jazmine allowed herself a small smile.

Because maybe… just maybe… there was more to fight for than the streets.

Chapter Forty-Two
"Final Strike"

The night felt heavier than usual — thick with a silence that screamed trouble.Jazmine's phone rang — no caller ID.

She answered cautiously.

Nothing but silence... then the faint sound of a baby crying.

Her blood ran cold. Jazmine's heart thundered as she swung open the door to J.J.'s room.

The soft glow of the nightlight flickered unevenly, painting ghostly shapes on the walls.

The bed was bare.

No sign of her son who had filled this room with life.

Her son's favorite blanket lay crumpled on the floor, tangled with a small pair of worn sneakers.

A stuffed bear, missing one eye, sat forgotten in the corner.

Her breath hitched, tightening in her chest like a noose.

"J.J.?" she whispered, voice breaking.

Only silence answered her.

Her eyes darted around the room — the closet door hanging open, the faintest scent of their last night's dinner lingering in the air.

Her pulse quickened as the reality hit like a freight train.

He was gone.

The door slammed behind her.

Trina stormed in, gun drawn, eyes sharp as daggers.

"They took him, Jazmine. The Cartel. This isn't just a message. It's a declaration."

Jazmine's knees nearly buckled, but fury blazed hotter than fear.

Her fingers clenched into fists, nails digging into her palms.

"This ends now," she growled.

The air thickened with tension, the safe house suddenly feeling too small, too vulnerable.

Her crew moved fast — weapons out, phones lighting up with calls, eyes hard with resolve.

Rico checked his gun with a shaky breath.Tone's usual calm was replaced with a tight jaw and clenched fists.

Trina's voice cut through the chaos.

"We hit back. Hard. We get J.J. back."

Jazmine's glare swept across them all — silent command.

No hesitation.

No fear.

Only war.

The clock was ticking.

Every second wasted could mean losing him forever.

She's, imagining her son's bright eyes looking up at her.

She wasn't just fighting for territory or respect anymore.

She was fighting for her son.

For her blood.

For the only thing in this world she truly loved.

Chapter Forty-Three
"Rescue Mission"

The city didn't sleep.

It prowled, watched, waited.

Jazmine stood over the map spread on the table, fingers tracing every route, every back alley, every place Miami's Cartel could be hiding her son.

Her crew circled the room — weapons loaded, eyes sharp, nerves tight.Trina leaned in, pointing at a cluster of docks known for cartel deals.

"This is our best shot."

Rico checked his ammo one last time.

Tone cracked his knuckles, eyes burning.

Jazmine's voice cut through the tension — cold, focused.

"We move fast. Quiet. No mistakes."

Every second without J.J. was a second closer to losing him forever.

They rolled out — black vans swallowed by the night as they slipped through Miami's maze of streets and shadows.

Jazmine's heart pounded with every mile.

Every siren.

Every turn.

They hit the docks — silent but deadly.

The Cartel's muscle was heavy, but Jazmine's crew was ready.

Gunfire erupted, echoing off the concrete and water.

Shots rang out — some close, some far.

Jazmine moved like a ghost — fast, fierce, relentless.

She pushed through the chaos, scanning every corner, every face.

Finally, in a shadowed warehouse, they found him.

K. J., scared but alive.

His eyes locked on hers — a silent promise passing between them.

Jazmine's breath caught.

This fight wasn't over.

But for now — she had her son back.Chapter Thirty-Eight — "Aftermath"
J. J. was safe.

But the city didn't pause.

The three-bedroom house felt both like a fortress and a cage.

Jazmine watched her son play in the yard, his laughter a rare light in a world of darkness.

But every shadow lurking beyond the fence whispered threats she couldn't ignore.

She held J.J. tight that night, the weight of her choices pressing heavy.

She wanted to shield him from the streets that nearly took him — but the war wasn't over.

Not by a long shot.

Her phone buzzed — another message from Miami.

A promise wrapped in threats.

Her enemies knew she was vulnerable.

Jazmine swallowed hard, steeling herself.

The fight for her son was a fight for her soul.

And she wasn't backing down.

Chapter Forty-Four
"Quiet Before the Storm"

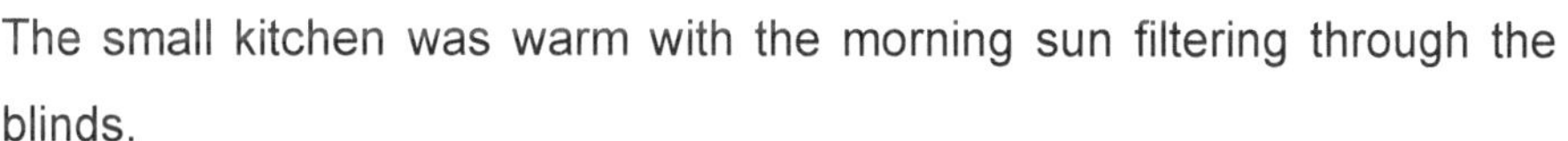

The small kitchen was warm with the morning sun filtering through the blinds.

Jazmine leaned against the counter, sipping black coffee.

Marcus sat across from her, calm and steady, a gentle smile playing on his lips.

They talked about everything and nothing.

About dreams beyond the streets, about hope, about J.J.

For a moment, Jazmine let her guard down.Marcus reached across the table, his hand covering hers.

"No matter what comes next, you're not alone."

Jazmine's eyes softened.

Maybe, just maybe, there was a way out.

Chapter Forty-Five
"The Queen's Gambit"

Jazmine stood in the shadows of the warehouse, eyes sharp, mind sharper.

She'd spent weeks gathering intel, turning allies, and setting the stage for a final strike.

Tonight, the Cartel wouldn't see her coming.

The crew moved in silently, every step calculated.

Jazmine's heart pounded with purpose — this was more than a battle for territory; it was for her family, her future.

Inside the warehouse, the Cartel's kingpins lounged, unaware their reign was ending.

Suddenly, the doors burst open.

Gunfire erupted.

Jazmine led the charge, unstoppable and fierce.

The Cartel fell one by one.

When the smoke cleared, Jazmine stood victorious — queen of a city she had fought to claim.

But victory came at a price.

Her phone buzzed — a new threat, darker and closer than ever.

Chapter Forty-Six
"Shadows Closing In"

The victory was still fresh, but the air felt heavier.

Jazmine paced her apartment, the glow of the city lights casting long shadows on the walls.

Her phone buzzed again — a text with no sender: "This isn't over."

She knew that voice.

Not Miami's Cartel… something darker.

Someone watching.

Waiting.

Her mind raced through every move, every ally, every possible enemy.

Trust was a luxury she no longer had.

That night, Jazmine sat with Marcus, her hands trembling slightly.

"I don't know how much longer I can keep this up," she confessed.

Marcus squeezed her hand.

"You're stronger than you know. And you're not alone."

But as the shadows closed in, Jazmine realized this was just the beginning of a new war — one that could destroy everything she fought for.

Chapter Forty-Seven
Final Showdown"

The city held its breath.

Jazmine stood on the rooftop, staring out at the skyline — a warrior poised before the storm.

Her crew gathered around, weapons ready, eyes fierce."This is it," she said.

"No more running. No more hiding."

Plans were laid bare, every angle covered.

Allies called in, traps set.

Her heart pounded, but her mind was clear — this was her fight.

As the night fell, the streets exploded into chaos.

Gunfire, sirens, and the roar of battle filled the air.

Jazmine moved like a force of nature, unrelenting.

When dawn broke, silence settled over the city.

The dust cleared, and Jazmine stood tall — battered, but unbroken.
Her phone buzzed.

A message from Marcus: "It's over. You did it."

She allowed herself a small smile — a moment of peace in a life that rarely offered it.

Chapter Forty-Eight
"Final Showdown"

The city's skyline burned orange as the sun dipped below the horizon.

Jazmine stood on the rooftop of a crumbling building, her eyes scanning the streets below like a hawk.

Her breath came steady, but inside, a storm churned — a mix of rage, fear, and resolve.

Behind her, her crew gathered quietly — Trina tightening her gloves, Rico checking his weapon, Tone stretching his fingers with a grim smile.

They looked to her — their queen, their anchor in this chaos.

"This is it," Jazmine said, voice low but ironclad."No more running. No more second chances."

Her words hung heavy in the cool evening air.

They moved out like shadows, slipping through alleys and side streets, every step calculated.

The plan was razor-sharp — traps laid, reinforcements on call, every angle covered.

Gunfire shattered the night's calm like thunder crashing over the ocean. Jazmine's heart pounded as she dove behind a dumpster, firing back with lethal precision.

Her world narrowed to the sound of shots, the heat of battle, and the faces of those she fought beside.

She could feel the weight of every bullet, every loss — the stakes higher than ever before.

Yet, in the chaos, her focus never wavered.

Every move she made was for J.J., for her crew, for the life she refused to lose.

Minutes felt like hours.

Sirens wailed in the distance, mixing with shouts and explosions.

The city was a battlefield, and Jazmine was its fiercest warrior.

When the dawn finally broke, the streets were silent except for the heavy breathing of survivors.

Jazmine stood on the rooftop once more, bloodied but unbroken.

Her gaze swept over the city she'd fought to protect — scars and all.

Her phone buzzed in her pocket.

A message from Marcus appeared on the screen:

"It's over. You did it."

For the first time in what felt like forever, Jazmine allowed herself a small, tired smile.

Maybe peace was possible after all.Epilogue — "New Dawn"

The sun rose soft and golden over the quiet neighborhood.

Jazmine stood on the porch of her small, three-bedroom house, breathing in the fresh morning air.

J. J. played in the yard, his laughter ringing like a melody she thought she'd forgotten.

Marcus stood beside her, hand warm in hers, eyes full of promise.

"This is just the beginning," he said.

Jazmine smiled, the weight on her shoulders finally lifting.

For the first time in years, she believed in something more — more than the streets, more than the war.

She believed in family, in peace, in a future where she could be free.

The past would always be a part of her — the battles, the losses, the scars.

But now, the dawn belonged to her.

And Jazmine was ready to live it.

NOTE

NOTE

www.ingramcontent.com/pod-product-compliance
Lightning Source LLC
Chambersburg PA
CBHW061101100726
47911CB00012B/341